Conjugating Hindi

Ishmael Reed

CONJUGATING HINDI

DALKEY ARCHIVE PRESS

Library of Congress Cataloging-in-Publication Data
Names: Reed, Ishmael, 1938- author.
Title: Conjugating Hindi / by Ishmael Reed.
Description: First Dalkey Archive edition. | Victoria, TX : Dalkey
Archive Press, 2018.
Identifiers: LCCN 2017057602 | ISBN 9781628972542 (softcover :
acid-free paper)
Classification: LCC PS3568.E365 C59 2018 | DDC 813/.54--dc23
LC record available at https://lccn.loc.gov/2017057602

www.dalkeyarchive.com
Victoria, TX / McLean, IL / Dublin

Dalkey Archive Press publications are, in part, made possible through
the support of the University of Houston-Victoria and its programs in
creative writing, publishing, and translation.

Printed on permanent/durable acid-free paper

In memory of Rose Mukerji

He forgot who he was, where he was, who else was there, and what was right or wrong.

The Mahabharata: A Shortened Modern Prose Version of the Indian Epic by R. K. Narayan

Noah said when he awoke: "Therefore it must be Canaan, your firstborn, whom they enslave. And since you have disabled me from doing ugly things in the blackness of night, Canaan's children shall be born ugly and black! Because you twisted your head around to see my nakedness, your grandchildren's hair will be twisted into kinks . . . because your lips jested at my misfortune, theirs shall swell; and because you neglected my nakedness, they shall go naked, and their male members shall be shamefully elongated! Men of this race are called Negroes; their forefather Canaan commanded them to love . . . fornication."

According to the translation of the commentaries in *Hebrew Myths: The Book of Genesis*

"This dude Mack is packing a tree trunk in his pants"

Comedian Leslie Jones in a skit trying to explain why a woman, played by Margot Robbie—considered attractive—is married to an ordinary-looking guy played by Mikey Day, *Saturday Night Live*, October 1, 2016

Chapter One

CALIFORNIA IS STILL THE world's biggest hideout. That's how it's described in a traditional California verse penned by an anonymous poet, "What Was Your Name in the States?"

> *Oh, what was your name in the States?*
> *Was it Muggins or Buggins, or Bates?*
> *Did you murder your wife*
> *And fly for your life?*
> *Say, what was your name in the States?*

Very few knew where Peter Bowman came from. Some said somewhere in the East. But wherever his origin, he had to get out of there fast. The administration of Woodrow Wilson Community College knew, but those files were confidential. Like many Californians, Bowman was fleeing something. He had arrived with the look of someone who had experienced a famine, but free from the force that debilitated him, he had gained weight. His teeth were no longer loose. And those that were missing were replaced with dental implants. He was regular again. His irises were no longer yellow, but white. No more blurred vision.

Peter Bowman, or "Boa," which was his nickname, was no different from the other faculty members who taught at Oakland's Woodrow Wilson Community College. He preferred it that way. He could elude his stalkers and "fly for his life." He was popular among his students and as a result of his history courses, where he would assume the poses of the historical personages being covered in the textbooks, he had a high enrollment. Like when he covered the Buffalo Soldiers who liberated Italian towns during World War II, often sent to the front without ammunition and commanded by Southern officers, he came dressed as a veteran. What a ham, in more ways than one. He loved to perform and at one time considered acting as a career. A bachelor, he bought his clothes at the Richmond Mall's Macy's and his idea of a vacation was a trip from Oakland to San Francisco, so parsimonious was he with the dollar. He'd check in at the Fairmont, his favorite hotel which was located off Union Square. Catch some Jazz at the SF JAZZ Center. An opera at the San Francisco Opera, perhaps having a dinner at the Hayes Street Grill, afterwards. (He only fell asleep once. He blamed it on Wagner's labored and tedious trombones.) Maybe a Broadway musical at the Orpheum. He sometimes visited MOMA, but no longer dined there. He had to put out some serious bread for something called an Apocalypse Burger.

It was no Big Mac. In fact it was like an overgrown hors d'oeuvre. He'd gone to see an exhibit of Edvard Munch's paintings. He and thousands of others. But Munch's *The Scream* wasn't shown. Though the information provided compared Munch to Van Gogh, Boa didn't buy it. Munch's subjects' eyes and hands were poorly drawn. The characters in his paintings could be those in the fiction of Fyodor Dostoyevsky. Blame it on Seasonal Affective Disorder. Long northern winters. His themes were those that one would find in a grade-B horror movie. He had more in common with Basil Gogos than Van Gogh.

Boa's forays into San Francisco didn't mean that he neglected Oakland, where he was now living. You might spot him at a concert given by the Oakland Symphony. In Jack London Square dining at Scott's, located on the Oakland Estuary. At Yoshi's listening to Jazz after having caught a movie at the Regal Jack London Stadium 9 across the street.

He spent his money at the places that hadn't been replaced by the Übers. He preferred the Old Oakland to the new Uptown Oakland, which was largely young, White, and artistic. He wasn't aware that the Millens were living and partying—at parties called "raves"—in hazardous warehouses until thirty-six artists were killed in a fire that took place at the Ghost Ship Warehouse. Just as the Oakland Hills fire of 1991 was blamed on a Black fire chief, a Black fire chief was scapegoated by the local media for the Ghost Ship Warehouse fire. Of course, it was more complicated than that. According to the Bay Area News Group, which won a Pulitzer Prize for its coverage of the fire, the police who had inspected the warehouse were also culpable, but to a lesser degree according to the press. "Police records show officers responded to an illegal rave and were warned that people were living at the warehouse almost two years before the deadly fire, yet did not cite anyone or forward the complaints to other city departments." Such was the power of landlords and developers that the lead developer among this group is referred to as Oakland's "real mayor." While some of the warehouse management, including the "master tenant," were hauled before a grand jury, such is the power of Oakland property owners and developers that the owner of the Ghost Warehouse came in for little criticism. She cared more about the upkeep of her white Mercedes than about supplying her property with sprinklers. "Chor Ng, the owner of the warehouse, was cited at least three times since 2009 for people living illegally inside a half-block of other properties she owned in East Oakland—the last of which occurred a week after thirty-six people died in the Fruitvale artists' collective on Dec. 2."

On March 27, at 2551 San Pablo Avenue, less noticed, Black residents Olatunde Adejumobi, 36, Ashantikee Wilson, 41, Edwarn Anderson, 64, and Cassandra Robertson, 50, were killed in a house located in an area of Oakland that a former White mayor had called "dysfunctional," and "Botswana," even though Botswana from some accounts had an enlightened leader who devoted earnings from the country's diamonds' money to building schools and shoring up the infrastructure.

The four who were killed in the West Oakland fire were trying to get their lives together. "More than eighty people used the building for transitional housing, but Urojas Community Services housed twenty-one people on the building's first and second floors. Urojas shared the first floor with another organization, House of Change." After the West Oakland fire, Keith Kim, the owner, who lives in the affluent Piedmont Hills, didn't show his face. The following is a report on how his tenants lived:

"The building's residents lived in horrific conditions: raw sewage leaks, rat, pest, and infestation, electrical defects, broken fire alarms and blocked fire exits," which was reported by *The East Bay Times* (April 25, 2017).

Darwin Bond Graham wrote: "Many of the West Oakland residents displaced by Monday's deadly San Pablo Avenue fire say that media outlets, the public, and city officials are downplaying, and even ignoring, the tragedy.

"Daryle Allums spoke to the *Express* and was blunt about why he thinks the fire survivors have drawn such little support: 'It's because the people we're dealing with are African American. People don't care.'

"Bobby Bishop, when asked why he thinks the city's assistance effort has been lacking, Bishop said, 'these are Black, African Americans. They don't give a fuck about us.'"

What the dead White artists and Black "dysfunctionals" had in common was that neither were welcome in the America of the 2000s. The ethnic cleansing of Oakland was begun by Jerry Brown, who, when mayor, envisioned 10,000 new residents inhabiting Oakland. *Street Spirit*, a newspaper distributed by the homeless, had warned in 2002 of the consequences of his Forest City Project that built upscale housing for the rich. They predicted that low income and homeless people "would not be able to live in the massively subsidized development."

Street Spirit was right. By October 2017, they were able to write: "For years, Oakland leaders wanted to make Oakland a hipster playground. They invested in making Oakland attractive to outsiders/gentrifiers. City planners courted businesses and

high-end condos that catered to them. Making Oakland
into a hipster playground meant whitening, or at least 'de-
blackening' Oakland. This would be necessary to attract more
white hipsters. They would even market the 'new Oakland.'"
Mayor Brown called his plan to bring 10,000 new residents
into Oakland "elegant density." Maybe the artists who were
killed in the Ghost Warehouse fire and the Blacks who'd been
displaced were inelegant? The homeless problem had become
so severe that by 2017 homeless cities were appearing beneath
every freeway in Oakland. Perhaps you would call them Jerry
Towns, after Jerry Brown who, with Wells Fargo, on a predatory
crime spree, was guilty of driving Blacks out of Oakland and
those remaining, out of their homes.

Like the Hobo jungles of the 1930s, tent cities were popping
up underneath the freeway overpasses. And during May, there
was a fire and their pitiful belongings were destroyed. It was

bound to get worse with the anti-poor policies of the new administration, which would reduce housing subsidies like Section
8. More people would end up homeless and in the streets. As
the work force was outsourced and even White workers were
replaced by robots, the country might deteriorate into chaos.
They could assuage the situation by giving the millions who

would be without jobs a Guaranteed Annual Income, which might amount to a small percentage of the GDP, but their greed blinded them to this solution.

This attitude toward the poor was not only obvious to "dysfunctional Blacks," but to those belonging to the middle class. Marvin X, a famous award-winning Black Nationalist poet, wrote:

> In our beloved city of San Francisco, we have been informed homeless shelters are filled with North American Africans, yes, until they are forced into the central valley towns so the gentrifiers can replace them in the cities, especially areas like Hunters Point, Fillmore and across the Bay in West Oakland (Former Oakland Mayor Jerry Brown, now Governor, said, "West Oakland is closer to San Francisco than San Francisco," meaning the West Oakland BART can get riders to San Francisco's financial district in five minutes, so they can maintain their pitiful lives of nothingness and dread, their world of make believe and conspicuous consumption.

The remaining San Francisco Blacks were being intimidated by the police, the method that New York used to expel Blacks. Moreover NextDoor.com, which was founded by the son of Indian immigrants, Nirav Tolia, was being used by the techie invaders to spy on Blacks, some of whom have lived in Oakland for decades. *East Bay Express* writer Sam Levin wrote: "White Oakland residents are increasingly using the popular social networking site to report 'suspicious activity' about their Black neighbors—and families of color fear the consequences could be fatal." Tolia denied the charges and claimed that he is committed to "small town" values. These "small town" values apparently include leaving the scene of an accident:

After allegedly attempting a dangerous lane change on Highway 101 in Northern California while driving his BMW X5 SUV, Nirav Tolia caused an accident that severely injured Patrice Renee Motley who was driving in her Honda Del Sol in an adjacent lane. Patrice's car went out of control, spun 180 degrees, crossed two lanes and hit the concrete median. Like Bollywood bad boy Salman Khan, Nirav Tolia too callously fled from the scene without stopping to help the victim.
(October 7, 2015, *Oakland Tribune*)

Another famous, internationally recognized artist—her work has been on exhibit at the Venice Biennale—was priced out of Berkeley. Sam Whiting told her story in *SF Gate* on January 6, 2017. Mildred Howard's mother had warned her: "Half a century ago," Whiting wrote, "artist Mildred Howard was given a warning by Mabel Howard, a well-known South Berkeley community organizer and activist: 'My mother said, "Watch. These people who are running away from us are going to get sick of commuting and come back, buy up this property and you won't be able to live here,"' Mildred Howard remembers her mother saying." Artists like Mildred Howard weren't the only ones who were being ousted as a result of Berkeley's Überization. *SF Gate* reported:

"Dozens of nonprofit organizations have made plans in recent months to leave downtown Oakland as commercial rents skyrocket, changing not just the neighborhood landscape, but where low-income children and families go to get basic services.

"Many of the nonprofits signed leases when building vacancies were high and the local economy was climbing out from the depths of the recession. With their agreements now expiring, organizations are seeing their rents nearly double."

But this wasn't just happening in Oakland. Artists and

Blacks were being driven out of cities across the nation by real-estate poachers. And flippers. Jeremiah Moss in his new book, *Vanishing New York: How a Great City Lost Its Soul*, according to *The Village Voice* "offers a wrenching, exhaustive chronicle of the 'hyper-gentrification' of New York—and the relentless monotony of chain stores and luxury high-rises that continues to suffocate small businesses and displace the poor, working-class, immigrant, and ethnic communities and artists, eccentrics, and bohemians who have made the city what it is."

The arts were still considered a frill by the middle class, which was ridiculed for its tastes in poetry, novels, films, cartoons, and every other medium. Take Yves' portrait of middle-class women in James Baldwin's *Another Country*:

> "I do not like *l'elégance des femmes*. Every time I see a woman wearing her fur coats and her jewels and her gowns, I want to tear all that off her and drag her someplace, to a *pissoir* and make her smell the smell of many men, the *piss* of many men, and make her know that *that* is what she is for, she is no better than that, she does not fool me with all those shining rags, which, anyway, she only got by blackmailing some stupid man."

They were weary of John Waters's square high school personnel in *Hairspray*; Chester Himes's Sugar Hill elite in *Pinktoes*; Frank Zappa calling Tipper Gore "a frustrated housewife." They will never forget that one. Nor will they forgive Murphy Brown and Mary Richards and others challenging their values. And what about Beyoncé's "All the Single Ladies," a hymn to pre-marital sex? In Stephen King's *It* middle-class mothers are domineering. The fathers slap their children in between guzzling beer while watching *77 Sunset Strip*. Tritone, the man devoted to classical Be-Bop, calling them square. Stoned Chelsea Hotel dwellers giggling furiously and passing joints and oatmeal cookies, while watching the Macy's Thanksgiving parade. Splitting their sides over the corny dance routines from the Broadway Musicals that survived the first few weeks after opening. But the ridicule of American middle-class values did not end with the generation of Waters, Baraka, Albee, and Warhol. The hip-hoppers extended their satire. Gave it deadly ghetto edge. Snoop Dogg standing over the corpse of President Trump on the cover of an album. The political arm of hip hop, Black Lives Matter, inspiring chapters in Brazil and elsewhere.

Cuban youth getting their information about the United States through hip hop. For Whites, the police were Tom Selleck. For Blacks, Browns, and Native Americans they were Harvey Keitel in *The Bad Lieutenant*. If middle-class members happened to hit the lottery, artists tricked them into paying millions for "art" that you could buy at your local Target for a few bucks. Ishmael Reed was one of those suckers. He used to sit and talk to Andy Warhol and Gerard Malanga at Max's Kansas City. He was so hip that he knew how Max's Kansas City got its name. Was photographed with Mickey Ruskin, owner of Max's Kansas City. But then he joined the gullible. He went and paid bucks to see Warhol's *Empire*.

There was a long tradition of the middle class being mocked by artists. The far-far Left had a long tradition of mocking their values, a series of cartoons that ridiculed them. Take this one by Russell Limbach. It's called "Reviewing Stand," published in 1934, in *The New Masses*.

Ain't that a scream! But now a new president, President Kleiner Führer, a billionaire, and the Developer-in-Chief, who pretended to be champion of the Middle Class, even though his heart was with the rich, was the vehicle for their vindictiveness.

As Bret Stephens wrote of these voters, "Every vote cast for Donald Trump was a vote for vulgarity. His supporters got exactly what they paid for." (July 28, 2017, *New York Times*). Even White progressives, traditionally the fiercest racism deniers, and both-sides-do-it pundits imputed noble motives to these voters, explaining their votes as a protest against "globalization," casting them as "forgotten Americans," who were concerned about "income inequality." Some pundits and commentators talked about their "cultural estrangement from the eastern elite." Two studies, however, and a book pointed to racism as the reason for their electing the worst president since Andrew Johnson, even if it meant his implementing policies that hurt them. Polls showed that President Kleiner Führer's supporters preferred Robert E. Lee over Obama and 20% said that Lincoln was wrong to free the slaves, yet Timothy Egan, a man who'd forgotten his ancestors, said that they were not racists and that the Democrats should abandon diversity and had been egged on by Black mischief—he didn't say that but that's what he and others mean by "identity politics." Blacks have been regarded throughout American history as the ones who put other groups up to mischief.

President Kleiner Führer gave the finger to the artists by including no inaugural poet during his inaugural ceremony and vowing to close the National Endowment for the Arts, and the artists paid him back with their poems, fiction, installations, and cartoons. They cringed as he decorated the White House so that it resembled a bordello. For writers like Jane Hirschfield, who recommended that banners including poems be included in the Science March, which was meant to get in the face of the Buckabees, who despised science, it was war.

Mass Slaughter

CHARLESTON CHURCH MASSACRE

Mass Shootings Prompt College to Drop Mascot's Name: Shooter

Shooting near Red Bluff is latest in a long list of firearm assaults in California

Appeal Offers Hope for Newtown Families in Suit Against Gun Companies

Not all Blacks had been driven from Oakland and Berkeley, or turned out into the rain. One of those who had survived the invasion of the Digitalites, Trollers, and Streamers was Peter Bowman, who belonged to a class of Black professionals. Given these circumstances, Boa and Obi and other Blacks were part of an elite. They didn't live in shelters. They weren't vulnerable to losing their health insurance like the millions—Black, White, Yellow, and Brown—who would lose their insurance under the policy of ethnic cleansing promoted by lawmakers who received large amounts from the insurance industry and whose leaders were guided by the Eugenics policies of Charles Murray, Ayn Rand, and the Alt Right.

But was he safe? He thought about the risks he was taking with his public appearances. His pursuers could find him. They could hunt him down. But then, he thought maybe he should leave California altogether. Of course, he couldn't return to the East where he was almost murdered by excessive affection.

Bowman and his class were better off than the Blacks who had been driven from Oakland by the banks, politicians, and developers. He had bought a house in North Oakland, one of the last Blacks to remain in the area which had been "farmed" by developers. It was a modest house of Italianate design. One bedroom. Kitchen. Living room. Parlor and a basement which also could serve as an apartment. Still, it wasn't enough room for the books that he brought from New York and so he put them in storage.

Bowman was a voracious reader. He had ready answers for some of the Whites who asked him the traditional questions asked of Blacks. *Was he behaving himself? Was he keeping out of trouble*, meant to be a harmless form of greeting, but which carried an undertow of hostility. He could always answer in the affirmative with a nod or a smile. Little did they know that he was a marked man. He was on the run. He was evading his pursuers by living a modest existence.

Abruptly, his fortunes changed. It all began with a lecture about William Monroe Trotter, a Civil Rights leader who was best known for his bitter opposition to Booker T. Washington, whose policies he considered accommodationist. But what made Trotter a hero to Blacks throughout the country was his confrontation with KKK admirer Woodrow Wilson.

On that day, Boa faced his class as usual after picking up an espresso from the campus cafe. Nodded to students who were strolling about in front of the campus buildings. Said hello to some who had been enrolled in his classes during previous semesters. He climbed the steps leading to his classroom and waited for his students to file in. Some brought their lunches and munched away noisily while he tried to lecture. Others talked. There was, however, a group of alert White, Black, and Brown students. Some of them were children or even grandchildren of '60s activists. They read books. They did their homework. Asked intelligent questions.

These were members of Boa's class who had been attracted to political hip hop. They were pretty astute when it came to alternative history. The Brown students were children and grandchildren of those who saw California and the Southwest as Greater Mexico, acknowledging the fact that this part of the country was taken by gunpoint and treaty violation. The Black ones wrote poems about police brutality. To them, Angela Davis and the Black Panthers were gods on earth. They were White students who read Howard Zinn and supported Black Lives Matter. They were Hispanic students who were familiar with Arte Publico Press's catalogue. They were Asian Americans who were familiar with the debate between Maxine Hong Kingston and Frank Chin. Native American students who could identify Harjo, Silko, Ortiz, Welch, Vizenor, and Donald Two-Rivers.

On that remarkable day, they took notes and nodded to one another when some new fresh information was revealed. He was lecturing about the tragic hero of the early Emancipation movement, Monroe Trotter, Civil Rights leader and editor of *The Boston Guardian*, and purported great-great grandson of Thomas Jefferson. White historians dispute this but these Black family oral histories are usually reliable. Besides, those who think that Jefferson was different from the other slave owners, who turned their plantations into their private harems, are usually ones who have a crush on the "great men" of American history. Enslavers. Indian fighters. Why else would slave traders like Alexander Hamilton and Andrew Jackson receive such exaltation? Andrew Jackson, who removed Creeks, Cherokees, and Chickasaws from their homeland? He was a slaveholder who tried to prohibit the distribution of abolitionist materials through the mails, and executed Seminole Indians without a trial. Would there be the musicals and coffee-table books devoted to their actions if they had enslaved White people? Benjamin Franklin, in his short story "Sidi Mehemet Ibrahim on the Slave Trade," treated this contradiction.

Boa trusted James Trotter's account more than those of the vaunted historians. Monroe Trotter's father, James, actually lived in the times that the historians write about.

James was credited with getting more pay for Black Union soldiers, and became Recorder of Deeds after Frederick Douglass resigned from the post. He inspired the young Trotter to study hard, agitate, and protest.

Boa talked about Trotter's bitter feud with Booker T. Washington, culminating in the Boston Riot, which was the name given to the incident when Trotter and others disrupted a speech that Washington had been scheduled to present at Mother Emmanuel Church. Trotter was jailed.

This didn't seem to excite the knowledgeable contingent of students, but when he talked about Trotter's facing down Woodrow Wilson in the White House and becoming so inflammatory that he had to be led from the people's house, they stirred. Trotter had confronted Woodrow Wilson about Wilson's re-segregating federal departments, even though Blacks and Whites had been working side by side for decades.

Some of these students leaned forward. The other students looked at him blankly. They were the White middle-class students who were victims of a curriculum that emphasized an archaic inquiry into an obsolete Europe. An overseas settler colony's version of Europe. Because of what they called "The West," meaning a few cities in Europe, they'd never heard of Fats Waller, Thomas Dorsey—the Gospel pioneer, Bette Davis, James Jones, Joan Crawford, Jack London, *The Grapes of Wrath*, *The Best Years of Our Lives*, *Sunset Boulevard*, James Cagney, Bill Robinson, Duke Ellington, the WPA choreographer Edith Segal, as well as Katherine Dunham, Martha Graham, Alvin Ailey and Pearl Primus, Jose Limon. Didn't know that Algebra came from the Arabs or that a Muslim scholar influenced Saint Thomas Aquinas. These individuals and institutions were dismissed by their elders, members of generations of teachers and scholars who accepted the same icons. Who never questioned the curriculum. They'd say a classic is something that is a century old. Some of the institutions and individuals about which they were ignorant had met that test or were approaching Classics status. William Wells Brown's *Clotel; or, the President's Daughter*, a book that combined fiction and nonfiction, was written in 1854. Ike Turner's "Rocket 88" was sixty-six years old. African-American Classical Music was over one hundred. "Fats" Domino was singing Rock and Roll in the 1940s when Elvis Presley was twelve years old or so, yet when he died at eighty-nine in 2017, Presley was mentioned in his *Times* obituary. Why? Does one rank one of Michelangelo's apprentices with Michelangelo?

The problem was that these were American icons instead of some obscure French king of the kind to which pages upon pages of the American textbooks were devoted.

At the end of the class, Boa got into his black Fiat and drove home. Thought little of the lecture that he'd delivered earlier and in fact was preparing the next lecture that had been listed in his syllabus. He was watching television when he saw one of his students being interviewed on the six o'clock news. His dinner had been delivered by one of a number of catering services that catered to Berkeley and Oakland residents. Boa leaned forward. His students were surrounded by some students from other Woodrow Wilson classes as well as surrounding schools and universities. They were demanding that the name of the school be changed from Woodrow Wilson Community College to Monroe Trotter Community College. The news cut to Charles Obi, former chair of Oakland's Jack London College, but now president of Woodrow Wilson. Charles Obi said that Woodrow Wilson had always been the name of the school and that would be the name of the school now and forever. Obi was a man of tradition.

When the administration led by Charles Obi resisted this demand, the students conducted a sit-in and a read-in where they read passages from Edwidge Danticat's essay, published in *The New York Review of Books*, about the horrendous effects of Wilson's invasion of Haiti. The Black students were joined by Hispanic, Asian, and White students. A rally was held in Frank Ogawa Plaza. Arrests were made. Since the eruption had begun in Bowman's classroom, he was interviewed by a local television station. He discussed the encounter between Trotter and Wilson. Wilson's praise for the pro-Klan movie, *The Birth of a Nation*. His interview was picked up by a major network. It went well and was a ratings hit. The next day, he received a call from Jack Sharkey of Columbia Speakers Bureau. Sharkey added Boa to his list of speakers. During the next months, he was in demand at colleges and universities and was making so much money that he began to indulge himself. Like having dessert with his evening meal. He knew that he was exposing himself to his pursuers, but the money was good. They delighted in the advantage that he had over other men, one that led him to live a profligate life in New York, one not of his choosing. At least he tried to convince himself that this was the case.

While he was able to hire a gardener to attend to his apple and apricot trees, Blacks were being exiled to former Sundown towns like Fremont, California. In some of these towns, they were welcomed with swastikas, nooses or racist scrawls on the walls of their homes. He was lucky. He could remain in the Berkeley, San Francisco and Oakland cities of Northern California and avoid the small California towns, which, for him, were Rod Serling country. In 1980, Oakland's African American population numbered 159,000, or 47 percent of the city's total. Thirty years later, it had shrunk to 109,000—28 percent.

He soon learned the tricks of the Public Intellectual trade. How to show up early in the Green Room while the bagels and cream cheese were fresh, and when the coffee container was still full. How to do a sound check. How to track the locations of cameras when being interviewed. Boa got so good that he began to dramatize the encounter, taking both Wilson's and Trotter's lines. He would strut up and down the stage as the audience sat in silence. Turn around dramatically. He'd wave his arms. Point a finger. Fold his arms. Pause with a dramatic silence. Then he'd turn dramatically, again. "And President Wilson, feeble and unable to stand, looked up at the young Trotter and with his voice in almost a whisper said, 'If this organization is ever to have another hearing before me it must have another spokesman. Your manner offends me.'" And then Boa would hobble around the stage imitating a weak Wilson, coughing, bent over, and drawing an imaginary shawl around his shoulders. Boa would give Wilson a faint voice. The kind that comedian Paul Mooney would give to a generic White and have Wilson utter to Trotter, objecting to Trotter's anger, those famous words "your tone, with its background of passion." And then he would perform the role of Trotter:

> "And Trotter, his eyes blazing from righteous indignation approached the president who was clearly frightened. It was a tense moment and some of the Secret Service men put their hands on their pistols whereupon Trotter held Wilson in chokehold.

The Secret Service men were prepared to shoot Trotter but the president told them to back off. (Given the tepid response to his earlier lectures, Sharkey had suggested that Bowman, in his words, Breitbart it up a bit. Nothing wrong with a little Factilying. A double vodka before his lecture helped. Besides, during President Kleiner Führer's administration, truth became what lay in the eye of the beholder.) 'The Black servant's eyes grew large like those of Willie Best's in *The Ghost Breakers*.

"The Secret Service men rushed Trotter. Trotter said: 'There's no need for you to put your hands on me, Gentlemen!' Again, Wilson told them to move away.

"And flummoxed by the kind of Black man to whom they weren't accustomed, they backed off. Trotter turned from the president who was sweating and breathing heavily and reaching for pills and a glass of water. Trotter held his head high. And slowly walked out of the White House. He was satisfied. He had shown the president a New Negro. One who would not cower. Educated. A Harvard man. Well off. The cherry blossoms were in bloom and their scent entertained his nostrils. He headed to the train station. He would take the train back to Boston. He slowly walked from the White House that had been built by slaves. Peeking at him through the curtains was that old Negro servant. He gave Trotter a smile. Trotter grinned."

These final lines would always earn a standing ovation. When the semester ended, Bowman requested retirement. He was forty-five. Still had black hair. Good muscle tone. But there was one part of his anatomy that had caused him nothing but trouble. He had worked long enough to earn a pension and medical coverage. As a public intellectual, he was in a position to earn more cash than was offered by Woodrow Wilson Community College. The head of the administration, Charles Obi, arranged for a farewell luncheon. Yes, Bowman had caused trouble for the administration, but the farewell luncheon was part of a tradition, and Obi was a man of tradition. Tall, with a face that featured prominent cat-like cheeks, with good posture and tailor-made suits. His family's story had been featured in *The Journal of Negro History*. He was educated at a Black historical college, where co-eds could walk through campus any time of the night without being molested.

"A lot of empty seats at the farewell luncheon," Boa said.

Obi glared at him. "What did you expect? This crazy crusade of yours all over the newspapers. You gave the college a black eye."

"How's that?"

"Not only did you get the Black students riled up but the White and Brown students as well. We've had a quiet campus. Computer and Business majors. They're no trouble. Kids who desire careers. Now you have aroused the radicals and anarchists. You're rewriting history. I can't understand why you can't let history go. A lot of dead shit. Dates and landmarks that nobody cares about."

"I just wanted to inform my students of what really happened. The facts. Not make believe. While the rest of the country might be entering a fact-free period, the campus should revere facts."

"Yeah, well all you did was obtain a lot of overtime pay for the Oakland Police Department. Then the students you inspired defaced the statue of Wilson that stands in the front of the school."

"The students had never heard of Monroe Trotter. He's the one who deserves the statue, not Wilson—."

"Man, motherfuck Monroe Trotter. The guy had to be difficult. Both Booker T. Washington and W. E. B. DuBois had issues with him. He finally committed suicide so troubled was his mental state."

"The cause of his death remains a mystery."

"Yeah, well, whatever. You wait until the college gets a Black president and then you do your militant shit. A middle-aged Hippie. Just like you clowns criticized President Obama when he was in office. Eighty-five percent of Black people supported Obama but you and the other fringe intellectuals nitpicked everything that he did."

By the time they reached Boa's Fiat, Obi had worked himself into apoplexy. He wouldn't even shake Boa's hand. But then, Obi, who had the reputation of a pragmatist, called out to Boa—

"Hey, Bowman?" Boa turned around before reaching the car. "Put in a good word to your Mom on behalf of the school."

"Yeah. Sure." People were always trying to get favors from his mother through him. He hadn't talked to his mom in a while. They had political and values disagreements. She was a widow. His father had died of prostate cancer. So had his grandfather, a Buffalo Soldier. The country had rewarded her for her service and she had climbed through the ranks and so she was one of these America First Black people. The country had been good to her.

Chapter Two

THE DIGITALITES HAD ALREADY named a store "The Brooklyn Bakery," as though we needed another Brooklyn. I happen to like Brooklyn, home of the Rome Neal family, but Brooklyn is OK where it is. There was also a new restaurant called "The Big Apple." The Millens were like those who participated in the Invasion of North America, who replaced the Indians' names with place names that connected them to their European hometowns. The current president, Kleiner Führer, had restored the invader's name for Mount Denali to Mount McKinley, named after a president whose only accomplishment was getting himself murdered in Buffalo. College Avenue, the Elmwood district's main drag, resembled Greenwich Village on a Saturday night. With bumper-to-bumper traffic. Cars full of Millens. Downtown chic restaurants and bars had replaced the older ones. No more Hofbrau. Esther's Orbit Room, where the Oakland Blues was born; shut down. "Paranoid" Ishmael Reed once wrote a poem about New York following him around "like a West Side Meat Packing house that will barter your heart for ice." He was talking about relocating to California from New York. A refugee from the New York 1960s. Now Oakland was beginning to look like Queens. But next to the early period of Oakland this amounted to an inconvenience. Yes, Black Panthers come into criticism because they were infiltrated by criminals and White armchair revolutionaries from the East, who wanted to manipulate them as one would characters in a videogame, but given Oakland's legacy the arrival of an armed Black self-defense organization was inevitable. Looking at

Oakland of today, it's hard to imagine that the KKK once ruled City Hall and burned crosses in Temescal Regional Park, which nowadays resembles the peaceable kingdom as Hispanic, Black, Asian, and Euro American picnickers gather there.

It was symbolic that Millens lived in a district named after the Elm tree. The Elm tree had been wiped out by Dutch disease, and for the Millens, the Black Civil Rights movement was also dead. It had been co-opted by something called "intersectionality." The only group that seems to have benefited from the movement was White women. Justice Sandra Day O'Connor gave Blacks a twenty-year deadline for Black Affirmative Action. For women (White) she required fifty percent. They were over fifty percent in college enrollment. A movement that had once been as strong as the Eucalyptus. In fact, the tree that was mentioned in the song, "like a tree standing by the water," must have been a Eucalyptus.

But now Digitalites had reached North Oakland, where Boa now lived. We all grew up on Wonder Bread. The Wonder Bread factory that was located on Adeline Street was now Bakery Lofts. And another sign of gentrification? A coffee shop opened around the corner from his house. And, of course, dogs. One invader, a tall shorts-wearing blonde, walked through the neighborhood with a Bloodhound on a leash. Given the historical relationship between Bloodhounds and Blacks this was an insult to the few Blacks remaining, whether she was aware or not. Tech sites like Pandora and Ask already had hubs located in Oakland, and Google was said to be scouting Oakland's naval yard for an office. Like the Delhi marketplace, in Jasbir Chatterjee's poem "Delhi Metro." Yes, like the Metro introduced modernity to India, but however clean it might be it could not insulate the city from "stray cows," and "maddening crowds." Bay Area Rapid Transit could not insulate its riders from the Blacks living among garbage at the Twenty-Seventh Street exit off 880. Like Delhi, gentrified Oakland and Berkeley had undergone a sleek Uptown makeover, with new restaurants, theaters, boutiques, but couldn't hide the misery of those who'd been left behind.

All that the Digitalites from San Francisco and New York knew about the Sixties was that it introduced some strains of Buddhism, Yoga, Macrobiotic food, (White middle-class) women's rights. Their hero wasn't Malcolm X. It was Alice Waters. And the successors to the underground newspapers, "alternative" newspapers that had been swallowed up by big chains, devoted whole supplements to where to eat, nothing about the forty million who had little or nothing at all to eat. And what would happen to the dwellers in the Jerry Towns if an earthquake hit. Where would they find food, water, and sanitation?

Californians were in a perpetual state of anxiety over the eight-point earthquake that would arrive within the next thirty years, or another cataclysmic fire. The film *San Andreas*, about the fault, which could generate a 9.5 earthquake, gave Boa nightmares. You never knew when one would hit. In fact, some were predicting that the Hayward Fault and the San Andreas Fault might erupt at the same time. Even scarier was a report from PBS's NOVA, which showed the left side and the right side of the San Andreas Fault moving away from each other at the rate of two inches per year. When the Pacific and North American tectonic plates grounded past each other, you didn't want to be around. That's why Californians are always on pins and needles. Moreover, California has always been a guest in North America, having originated in South America. It is a geological freak. Here you find soil, plant life, minerals, and fossils not found in the rest of the United States. You didn't want to be around when California decided to relocate, maybe ending up in the Pacific. Suppose that geological California decided to go home?

Eucalyptus trees, because of their oil content, had been

blamed for the fires which swept the hills' neighborhoods in 1991. They were still there. Brought to California in the nineteenth century by Aussies—who were just as rugged—they were now classified by biologists as pariah trees. FEMA was about to implement a plan that would destroy the trees. But the pesticides that they planned to employ to end the menace for all time were carcinogenic. The people in the Oakland Hills had to choose their poison.

With the insurance settlements, they had replaced their homes with even bigger ones, narrowing the streets even further, which would make it even more difficult for fire equipment to reach their homes if another such fire occurred.

And with the drought, hotter summers were unavoidable. Each summer after the year 2000 was breaking all heat records. Boa's plan was to spend one more year in California, about the time when the water emergency would become so dire that there would be water riots. He was looking for another place where he could hide, and given the neo-Nazi clique that now inhabited the White House—maybe Costa Rica? In 2015, each resident was limited to thirty-five gallons per day. Another year and you wouldn't get a bird's bath worth of water unless El Niño intervened but suppose the drought continued after El Niño? Besides, the drought had been so severe that even an El Niño would not make up for the water that was needed. What then? Big Agri was hogging all the water, siphoning off eighty percent of the precious liquid. Because of the heavy rains of December 2016, some were predicting that the drought had ended. And even with the rains that came in the winter of 2017, the Governor warned that the drought hadn't ended. The *L.A. Times* editorial page wasn't so sure. California was a land of extremes. Too much water, too little water. Deserts and rainforests. Condors and scrub jays. Ronald Reagan, Richard Nixon, Sam Yorty, the Knowlands, but also Tom Hayden, Huey Newton, Robert Maynard, and Sheriff Hennessy.

Despite all that December rain and snow, the year's first
official measurement found that the water in the crucial
Sierra snowpack hovers at around two-thirds of the
historical average for early January.
(*L.A. Times*, January 6, 2017)

They were predicting that the drought would last for a hundred years.

Then there was the matter of the West Nile Virus. With the lack of water, mosquitoes and the birds that they affected were more likely to share the same pools of stagnant water. The deaths arising from persons infected with this disease were rising.

Maybe it wouldn't be so bad if people would not only avoid dairy and meat products but also stop eating nuts. Hazelnuts and walnuts consumed 1,260 gallons of water to yield a pound and 1,112 gallons to yield a pound, respectively. And get this. Six-hundred and sixty gallons of water to produce one hamburger!! The Millens weren't aware that in the forties and fifties when industries employed millions of workers, the homeless population was confined to White male alcoholics, at least this was the case in Buffalo, New York. They dwelled in the downtown area near the waterfront. Some argue that the homeless situation began with the Reagan administration. When Governor of California, he closed the mental hospitals and sent the patients to the streets to fend for themselves. Could Reagan's coldness be traced to the relationship between the former president and his alcoholic father? Could his father's alcoholism be traced to the haunting of his generation by The Great Famine? And could some of the meanness shown by Irish-American members of President Kleiner Führer's administration be traced to the famine? One of his biographers mentions a revealing anecdote. Reagan came home one day to find his father drunk. Lying outside in the cold. Reagan said that he didn't know whether to leave him there, or take him indoors. He decided to take him indoors. The mental patients weren't so lucky. He turned the mental patients out into the cold. Arnold Schwarzenegger, when Governor, had an opportunity to bring the homeless indoors, but instead gave yacht owners a break with the money meant for providing the homeless with shelter and then, to flaunt this callous move, showed up at a yacht show. As a newspaper put it: "Program for mentally ill eliminated."

> SACRAMENTO – Making good on a promise to trim the state budget, Gov. Arnold Schwarzenegger eliminated a $55-million program Friday that advocates say has helped thousands of mentally ill homeless people break the costly cycle of hospitalization, jails and street life . . . despite the allegedly strapped conditions of the state, legislators managed to preserve a tax break for some purchasers of yachts, planes and recreational vehicles—a measure that could cost the state as much as $45 million.
> Los Angeles Times, August 25, 2007
> Scott Gold, Lee Romney, and Evan Halper

Trashing the poor was an alien idea to Boa, who, like Chappie Puttbutt, had grown up in the American Army where having one another's back was the culture. Like Puttbutt's, both Boa's father and mother were army careerists. They grew up in a time when there were few options for bright Black people. They chose military service. Though they moved a lot during his childhood, he was well cared for and received a good education. And now, because of his sudden fame, he was able to do improvements on his North Oakland house, which was located on a block that, previously, was 95 percent Black. The American automobiles of the middle-class Blacks, who had resided in this neighborhood, had been replaced by BMWs, Fiats, Volvos, Toyotas, and expensive cars like Cadillac Escalades. Instead of gunshots at night, one heard the constant drilling and hammering during the day as flippers repaired these old houses so that they could sell them at astronomical prices. They had turned his block into an industrial zone. Don Peralta, former leader of the California Assembly, had said in a correspondence that there were two Oaklands. Some of the Blacks who'd been left behind were living in third-world conditions while the Übers were dining in outdoor cafes.

Chapter Three

BOA'S MORNING ROUTINE WAS to fetch the newspapers while the Guatemalan coffee was brewing. Then he would rest in bed while reading the three newspapers to which he subscribed. Then the Internet. He was old-fashioned. After devouring the editorial and sports pages, he turned to the news. The headlines were about Carol Christo, the Cuban American presidential candidate's wife, caught smuggling cocaine into the United States. She pled that the cocaine didn't belong to her but was placed in prison anyway. Before her family could put up a bond, she hanged herself. For her, a member of a distinguished Cuban American family, whose ancestors had come to the States from Castro's Cuba, such humiliation was a disgrace. His career ruined, Christo resigned from Congress and retired from public life.

The Indian right-wing intellectual Shashi Paramara had made a film about the congressman's praising Mexican General Santa Anna as the Mexican "Abraham Lincoln" in a student paper. The paper was based upon an excerpt from a letter that Santa Anna wrote to the Mexican Minister of War. Santa Anna had written:

> *Greater still is the astonishment of the civilized world to see the United States maintain the institution of slavery with its cruel laws to support it and propagate it, at a time when the other nations of the world have agreed to cooperate in the philanthropic enterprise of eradicating this blot and shame of the human race.*

Santa Anna freed slaves who were being held by the settlers who had invaded Texas. Paramara's billionaire backer paid for ads describing the senator as someone who supported the assassin of American folk hero, Davy Crockett, who had come down in American folklore as "King of the Wild Frontier." Christo's dissertation was that Crockett and others were defending slavery at the Alamo.

Even though Christo was a member of the far Right and opposed to immigration, the Benefactor, a New York Hedge Fund billionaire, and his friends, were dead set against a Hispanic presidency, which would unify North America with South America, according to them, and send Whites scurrying to New Zealand or Europe, which was already being overrun by Arabs and Africans. Poet Victor Cruz was even saying that the United States was a recent construct and when an early mapmaker coined the term America, he meant Brazil. Is the United States an Invisible Empire? The Benefactor retweeted the White Genocide blog a lot. When told that the Cuban American senator was opposed to immigration, gay rights, and condemned abortion even in cases of incest and rape, the Benefactor and his circle of billionaires said that Christo's conservative principles were phony and once elected he would move to unite North and South America under Hispanic rule and that Whites would be deported. With the steady rise of the Hispanic birth rate, Blacks might become "the model minority." Again. The Benefactor instructed his newspaper editors to refer to Christo as a Manchurian candidate. A Trojan Horse. His media personnel, some of whom were hired for their central casting looks, followed his orders with their usual "yes Massa" to the rich. They didn't want what happened to Dan Rather to happen to them.

Though of Hispanic ancestry himself, Christo was opposed to migration to lands out of which the Mexicans were chiseled by the administration of James Polk, a slave owner.

Another item that caught Boa's eye was about an Indian family that was suing the British Crown for the child abuse committed by Lord Mountbatten. He then turned to local news. Crowds showed up at Oakland City Hall protesting a high-rise "luxury tower" on Twelfth Street. Boa appreciated Oakland's horizontal skyline, but with the invasion of developers who lived as far away as Hong Kong and Israel, that would change. He was at peace living in North Oakland, despite the monitoring by his new neighbors who were subscribers to NextDoor.com, which had the backing of one hundred million dollars from venture capitalists, many times the budget of the former East German secret police, which had the same assignment. Its name was Stasi. Of course NextDoor, an organization of Whites who use an Indian as the spook-who-sat-by-the-door, wasn't the only one dedicated to keeping tabs on the movements of Blacks. In Los Angeles, a Latino gang called "Big Hazard" was indicted for firebombing the homes of Blacks so that they would move from the Ramona projects. "The twenty-five-page indictment unsealed Thursday alleges that a sophisticated level of planning went into the attack and describes Big Hazard's longstanding efforts to scare African Americans away from the project. Gang members would 'monitor the activity' of African Americans and threaten those who lived in Ramona Gardens 'that they risked harm if they remained,' according to the indictment." That was one aspect of Hispanics (millions of whom were Black given the plantation's "one drop rule") and traditional African Americans. Black, Hispanic, and White prisoners joined to strike against the California prison system, called by one author "The Golden Gulag." This cooperation between Blacks and Hispanics was little noticed by the media. The colonial policy is to divide and conquer. North Koreans against South Koreans. Muslims against Hindus, Tutsis against Hutus, Hispanics against Blacks, etc.

During the month of February, Black History Month, when Black intellectuals, writers, and performance artists added much-needed funds to their annual incomes, a windfall of cash landed in Boa's lap. Like contestants in a show where they are invited to shop for a limited length of time and able to keep all of the valuables that they could grab during that time, Black writers, painters, and photographers were in demand during those twenty-eight days. During the remaining eleven months, however, White writers, artists, playwrights, and television scriptwriters—people who had never been profiled, racially, or red-lined—occupied the profit end of the Black Experience. But now these writers were beginning to encroach upon February, the month during which Black writers could hustle. One leading Book Review recommended books about Blacks written by White authors for Black History Month.

This list showed that not only were live Whites making a profit from the Black Experience, but the estates of dead White writers were getting paid. According to *The New York Times*, April 19, 2017, the same situation was occurring elsewhere, "While the number of children's books featuring African-American characters has grown in the last decade, the number of books by Black authors has barely budged, according to data collected by the Cooperative Children's Book Center at the University of Wisconsin-Madison's School of Education. Out of some 3,400 children's books published in 2016, 278 featured Black characters, up from 153 in 2006. *But only ninety-two of those books were written by Black authors, roughly the same number as a decade ago.*" So what goes as the Black Experience in publishing, theater, film, television is determined by those who were never the victim of a capricious traffic stop, or startled the waiters and waitresses as they entered the breakfast area of an upscale Santa Monica hotel, or were directed to the delivery floor when they visited their Park Avenue lawyer. And those who determine the commercial trends in Black culture will always have the bottom line in mind.

There were scores of Black, Hispanic, Native American, Asian American writers who like Elizabeth Nunez found themselves limited in their access to readers as a result of intervention by "outsiders." Even the ones who were selected as tokens had to engage in sororicide and fratricide—the battle royal—because only one at a time could survive. Boa was searching for a solution. A way that would deliver him from an artistic mosh pit. One day, the opportunity arrived.

Chapter Four

HE GOT AN URGENT message from Jack Sharkey of Columbia Speakers Bureau. He asked Boa to fly to New York. Said he didn't want to discuss an important matter on email or the phone. Boa flew from Oakland airport on JetBlue to New York and met his agent in his office on Fifth Avenue. Sharkey had some pretty famous clients on his list. Movie stars. Public intellectuals, captains of industry, and even a couple of ex-presidents. Jack was a multimillionaire. He was wearing an expensive suit. A diamond earring. Was one of these fast talkers. For Boa he sent out for deli sandwiches. Later Boa heard that he took Shashi to the kind of place where if you summoned a waiter, thirty people would show up and the daily menu was read aloud in flawless French. He offered him a seat after Boa was escorted into his office. He recognized some of the photos on the office's wall. Famous individuals in frames that included their autographs.

"How was your flight from Oakland?" Maybe he'd been approached by a publisher about Boa doing a biography of Monroe Trotter. After all it was his comments about Woodrow Wilson and Monroe Trotter on television that made him a public intellectual in demand, regardless of how this informed his stalkers of his whereabouts.

"It was okay. They have Wi-Fi. I watched CNN during the entire trip."

"Where do you live in Oakland?"

"Near Children's Hospital. We don't get much sleep. The hospital's ambulances are constantly heading up our block. Helicopters landing on their landing pad."

"My oldest son lives in Oakland. He's been living there for about six months. He has begun the Oakland Heritage Foundation for Artists." Some of the longtime Oakland residents were complaining about outsiders arriving from New York and receiving more grant money for their projects than those Oaklanders who had been living there for decades.

"I guess you're wondering why I summoned you here."

"Yes."

"We've made some nice money from your lectures. There's an opportunity for you to make some more money. You'll be able to break out of the Black History Month ghetto," *which was also being gentrified*, Boa thought.

"How's that?"

"You heard of Shashi Paramara?"

"Yeah. I saw what he did to the Cuban American presidential candidate. Found a paper that he wrote in college praising Santa Anna as the Mexican Lincoln. And then his wife was found smuggling cocaine. She hanged herself in a prison cell she was so disgraced. The guy was ruined. It's all over the news."

"Yeah, that was unfortunate—"

"And he then got into trouble being caught in bed with a preacher's wife by leaders of that Christian college where he was dean."

"Yeah, well Shashi can be pretty sloppy when it comes to pussy, but the Christian college's firing him was a blessing in disguise. He was removed from the dreary dull life of faculty teas and became an overnight celebrity after he wrote that op-ed column about the candidate, Christo."

"Yeah, calling Christo a Trojan Horse. Once in a while, I've caught him on the Sunday shows. His comments about global trends in finance and politics. Got caught in a plagiarism scandal, right?"

"The same."

"What about him?"

"He's looking for a debating partner. I mentioned your name as someone who could fill the spot."

"What will we be debating?"

"He's going to defend the institution of slavery. Your job is to take the opposite point of view."

"Defend the institution of slavery!! What the fuck are you talking about?"

Boa rose and in a rare exhibit of anger threw his napkin to the table.

"Relax. Sit down. Slavery is hot. A big money maker. Look at all of the books, movies, and TV documentaries about the subject. Torture porn and oppression chic? They brought back *Roots* for heaven's sake. HBO is going to do a fantasy series imagining what would have happened if the South had won the war. It's called *Confederate*."

"What do you mean *IF* the South had won the war? You have admirers of John Wilkes Booth in Congress. A majority leader who nullified everything that the Black president attempted.

President Kleiner Führer is surrounded not only by a cult of neo-Confederates but even Nazis. A president who has expressed his admiration for mass murderers and rebels."

"You get ten thousand per debate. Plus travel, lodging, and honoraria."

Boa was obviously getting agitated.

Jack Tells Boa That He Can Make Some Money From The Slavery Culture

Boa sat back down. He became quiet.

"Of course, Shashi will get more money. He's famous. Plus he received the prestigious V. S. Naipaul Award. This will get you cash all year around instead of just for February." Ignoring the slight, *ten thousand dollars,* Boa thought.

"Now, most of our audience members will be White. Most probably conservative. So a lot of bombast from you will turn people off. Your positions have to be enunciated coolly but firmly. Of course, you don't have the intellectual chops of Shashi. And please avoid those dreadful Identity Politics. A real turnoff. As you know, he was educated at one of those English boarding schools. You can say things like 'we can agree to disagree.' Shashi will have better accommodations than yours. He'll ride first class. You'll ride coach. Look at it this way. In film they have a character who is the sidekick of the star. That's kinda like what your role will be. Comprende?" He looked away. Then examined his watch as though he had little time to spend with Boa.

"I don't know. Slavery was one of the worst violations of human rights in history. To use it as entertainment would be demeaning. Besides, I'm a role model for many of my students. My appearing on a show which has the title 'Was Slavery All that Bad?' might be misconstrued. Especially if there's money involved." Boa was clearly angry. His heart began to beat, rapidly.

"Be reasonable. Yes, you'd be making money but at the same time you will remind the world so that such a human catastrophe will never happen again."

"I don't know. It doesn't seem right. Why didn't you get Chuck Skippie? Something like this is right up his alley. He could argue both pro and con if the price is right."

"We couldn't meet his price. Besides, he's rolling in dough from that *Trace Your Steps* show he moderates. You know the one where he tells stars about their ancestry."

"I don't know. It sounds too much like the commercialization of a human holocaust."

"Look, Boa. I don't need an answer until Monday. Go back to Oakland. Sleep on it." After finishing their knockwurst sandwiches, his secretary brought coffee. Supermarket coffee. Not the fancy espresso Sharkey provided for Shashi and his entourage. During the luncheons that Sharkey threw for Paramara and his assistants, espresso was served from a silver tray. In cups made of china.

He tossed about in his mind the reaction that would occur were he to tour the country debating the evils of slavery with Paramara, who had said some terrible things about Blacks, gays, and women. Moreover, Paramara was writing a book for a Broadway musical about Robert E. Lee, *The General Who Rocked*. The producers wanted to make the same kind of money as *Bloody Bloody Andrew*, which glorified the president regarded as the Eichmann of America's Indian policy, and *Hamilton*, in which Alexander Hamilton, a slave trafficker, was shown as an "abolitionist and progressive."

In fact, Native Americans protested the Off-Broadway production that glorified Jackson, which was given five stars by some of the country's leading critics. Rihana Yazzie, a playwright who helped organize a protest of the Minneapolis production, said the musical "reinforces stereotypes" and left her feeling "assaulted."

"The truth is that Andrew Jackson was not a rock star and his campaign against tribal people—known so briefly in American history textbooks as the Indian Removal Act—is not a farcical backdrop to some emotive, brooding celebrity," Yazzie wrote in an open letter. "Can you imagine a show wherein Hitler was portrayed as a justified, sexy rock star?" She left out the part about Jackson owning 144 slaves and how inventive he was in covering up the brutal treatment of his slaves. Joy Harjo, the poet, also objected to this ajaxing of "Old Hickory" by Public Theater with its *Bloody Bloody Andrew Jackson*.

"I walked out of the show and protested. My seventh-generation grandfather Monahwee fought against Andrew Jackson for our rights, our homeland. In the show he was a weakling, a yes man, and gave land away."

The producers of *Robert E. Lee, The General Who Rocked* were aware of the protests that might occur were they to mount the show. But such protests would be countered by the establishment critics who would inflate the ticket prices for the show by heaping the same kind of praise on the Lee musical as they did with genocidal murderer Jackson and slave trafficker Alexander Hamilton. Besides, Robert E. Lee has always had followers both in the North and the South. They can take down all of the Confederate flags in the South and pull down the statues of Jefferson Davis like they pulled down the statue of Saddam Hussein, but Robert E. Lee's reputation as the noble underdog who fought in an epic Romantic battle will survive. Frederick Douglass complained about it at the time: "We can scarcely take up a newspaper that is not filled with nauseating flatteries of the late Robert E. Lee . . . It would seem from this that the soldier who kills the most men in battle, even in a bad cause, is the greatest Christian." But these times were different. The new president, whom Gail Collins called "a nut job," had two sons. Comedians were calling them "Beavis and Butthead." The Butthead son had gone to Mississippi, where he praised the Confederate flag as part of Southern tradition.

But there were enough bucks behind *Robert E. Lee, The General Who Rocked* that whichever protests challenged its Broadway run would be greeted with sneers about political correctness, this stuck record of a charge used against the left by the right who borrowed the phrase from the Communist Party. Predictably, William Kristol said that we should honor and respect Robert E. Lee, who had a whipping post installed at his home at Arlington, which became a burial place for veterans, which, some say, was done to spite an American traitor. Perhaps the Rockefeller Foundation, which bought tickets for *Hamilton* so that school children could attend a musical about a slave trafficker who even left a note about negotiating a slave purchase for $225.00, would possibly pay for school children to see the Lee musical too.

After his marriage, Hamilton intervened to retrieve his in-law's slaves. In 1784, his sister-in-law Angelica wrote

*to her sister Elizabeth explaining that she wanted her
slave, Ben, returned. In response, Hamilton wrote to
John Chaloner, a Philadelphia merchant who conducted
business transactions for Angelica's husband, and stated,
"you are requested if Major Jackson will part with him
to purchase his remaining time for Mrs. Church and to
send him on to me." In addition, Hamilton also handled
Angelica's husband John Barker Church's finances because
the couple spent most of their time in Europe. Hamilton
deducted $225 from Church's account for the purchase of
"a Negro Woman and Child."*
*(http://www.earlyamerica.com/early-america-review/
volume-15/hamilton-and-slavery/)*

He stepped out into Fifth Avenue. Given the Manhattan-
ization of Oakland, he could imagine that soon there would be a
part residency, part business development in his neighborhood.
Maybe a coffee shop, a restaurant, an organic supermarket, and
a Pilates business located on the first floor. They'd call it The
Fifth Avenue. On the plane from JFK to Oakland, he mulled
over the decision about whether he would take Sharkey's invitation. He went to sleep in economy. When he awoke they were
flying over Salt Lake City. When he stood up from his seat,
he almost collapsed because there was such little leg room that
his legs had become numb. They were about two hours from
landing in San Francisco. When Boa arrived home he found a
letter from the United States Treasury. He was being audited.
He could pay $60,000 or bring all of his receipts, etc. to the
audit. He called Monday and told Jack Sharkey that he would
take the job.

Chapter Five

AFTER HE AWOKE THE next morning he checked his online bank balance. $5,000 of the $10,000 had been deposited. This was exhilarating! He went over to the closest Peet's and bought coffee. This particular Peet's, located between Telegraph and Shattuck, a few doors down from the Genova Deli, which closed after eighty-one years, was a hangout for members of the Eritrean community, who were sitting at tables indoors and outside perhaps discussing the latest cruel antics of the dictator, Isaias Afwerki, who had jailed eleven top government officials and banned seven independent newspapers. One of these African dictators who wouldn't yield power. He noticed two men sitting in the corner, chatting away. One was Ishmael Reed, the author, and the other was Chappie Puttbutt, son of two generals. Chappie had become a hero when he fought successfully against a takeover of Jack London University by Japanese investors. On the day that the crisis ended students carried him on their shoulders while shouting "U.S.A., U.S.A.! We're # 1. We're # 1." He had taken a buyout. Rumor was that he'd received a number of grants to write books about nineteenth-century Black authors. Instead of writing the books, he took the money and invested in the stock market and financed vacations to St. Thomas and St. Lucia. Those with little knowledge of Black literature and who were dependent upon scouts to tell them about the subject had provided him with patronage that was supposed to go to writers and artists. Instead he gave awards to his former colleagues.

Boa walked up to their table. "Mind if I join you?" Chappie

rose and shook his hand. Ishmael Reed kept his place. His hair was almost completely gray. He bore a black bruise on his forehead which he got from slipping on a waxed kitchen floor. At 79, he was falling maybe two times per year. But unlike other septuagenarians, he fell in elegant places. Like slipping on the ice at Sils Maria in the Swiss Alps. He looked up at Boa. Though he had received more grants and royalties than at least 75 percent of American writers, he was still kvetching. Grousing. Hyperventilating. Seems that the older he gets the more he thinks of himself as a Black Panther because of a draft of a poem that Langston Hughes dedicated to him but now there were certainly signs of deterioration. Chappie said, "I've been trying to tell Reed here that it's not his fault that slavery has become big business. He just finished interviewing me for his magazine *Konch*." And Boa saw Reed's iPhone lying on the table, which had been recording the interview. Known for detecting cultural trends and reaping rewards from them, Chappie was now "post-racial." Chappie had published a new book entitled *What If I Prefer Beethoven Over Coltrane?* Reed was going to print the interview in his magazine, *Konch*, run by him and his daughter, Tennessee. Chappie had gained a lot of weight. His face had taken a hit. Misshapen with fat. Dark rings about his eyes. Yellow teeth. He was partying a lot. Spending his summers at Lionel Hampton, the name that Whites gave to the Black enclave in the Hamptons.

"Look at this," Reed said, indignantly, pushing *The Wall Street Journal* toward him. It was opened to the business page. (Another sign of gentrification, free sample copies of *The Wall Street Journal* were being distributed in neighborhoods that were formerly Black.) The headline was "Chains Soar." Subtitle: "More Gains For Bondage, Inc.!" Bondage, Inc. was a multi-billion dollar corporation that promoted books, films, Broadway musicals, operas about slavery.

"So what does this have to do with you?

"I started the whole thing," Reed said, "when I wrote *Flight to Canada*. I called it my 'Neo-Slave Narrative.' Now the whole thing has gotten out of hand. It's become a big racket. Novels, movies, musicals, and hundreds of non-fiction books. Some of their creators are making more money revisiting slavery than some of the slave owners who actually owned slaves. In fact, in one of the movies, African actors, who might be descendants of those who sold Blacks into slavery, are performing as traditional African Americans in a movie about slavery. One can say that their families are getting paid twice for their role in the slave trade."

"Excuse me," Reed said, eyes darting about frenetically like those of John Brown played by Raymond Massey. He got up and went to the restroom. At his age, he was going to the restroom a lot.

Chappie Puttbutt whispered to Boa, "The guy is really losing it. In his book *Flight to Canada*, he has a poem keeping ahead of the character Robin Quickskill and now he's saying that this book—his own book—is tracking him."

"What do you mean?" Boa asked.

"He's spending time in Montreal and other places in Canada like Quebec City. He just got back from Toronto. His last three books were published in Montreal. Le St. Sulpice Hotel, a Montreal hotel, even uses a poem of his that they commissioned in their brochure. He calls himself a Black writer in exile. For all who would hear, he talks about buying two four-bedroom, three-bath homes in Canada for the amount that he's paying for one here. The only exile he knows is that he no longer goes to the Peet's coffee shop on Shattuck in Berkeley, and instead is coming here."

"Why did he stop going there?"

"He was profiled racially."

"In progressive, liberal Berkeley?"

"He says that he went to order a double espresso and when

it came time for them to take his order, the White woman who had been serving other customers stepped aside and a Black man took his order. He says that the same thing happened at Starbucks at the mall in Emeryville across from Trader Joe's. He says that Berkeley and Oakland are creating employment for Black men by having them racially profile other Black men and when these spies are not available they assign Chicanos to do the job. He says that he walked into the Berkeley Bowl one day, where the Hispanic women know his order for espresso without his requesting it. On this particular day, a couple of Hispanic men had taken their place. He said that they fussed so much over the White couple who were next in line that they forgot his order."

"So how does Reed feel about these slights from Colored immigrants?"

"He says that they still haven't unburdened themselves of a Colonial mentality, even though they come from nations in Africa, the Middle East, and South America that have been independent for decades."

"Well how is he going to feel about me?"

"What do you mean?"

"I've signed up to debate Shashi Paramara. You heard of him?"

"Seen him on television. One of those right-wing Indians who is being used against the brothers and sisters. I saw one of them, a short, chubby woman on MSNBC. Her last name was Metha or something. She told the Black panelists on the same show, 'My parents came over here and began a mom and pop store. They sent me to college. What is the problem with Blacks?'"

"Yeah, well they want me to debate him."

"Debate him about what?"

"Was Slavery All That Bad?" Chappie didn't react.

"You don't seem upset?"

"Everybody is getting paid. Why not you? I get pegged as a person without principles. Even my parents accused me of waving my finger in the wind to determine which way the cultural and political winds were moving. You remember at Jack London, I played the conservative thing because I thought that the university would grant me tenure. That they would see me as someone who would go along to get along. A team player. Someone who was collegial. But then when I was denied, I went to the other extreme. The Japanese who were flying high during that period had, through a large endowment, taken over the university. Coincidentally, Dr. Yamato, who became the president, was tutoring me in Japanese. He appointed me his right-hand man and I used it as an excuse to take revenge upon those who had denied me tenure."

"I read about it," Boa said.

"I found that the Japanese could be just as Xenophobic as those who call themselves Eurocentric. I sought solace in religion. First Eastern, but dropped that after I heard a speaker use the phrase 'the sea of awareness.' I didn't want to be a member of a religion whose representatives talked in such a hokey fashion. I moved on to a religion that has no one invoking his or her gods on the battlefield. But I abandoned that one after they announced that they were going into the California countryside to sacrifice a goat. Since then I have become an agnostic in politics, an agnostic in religion, and an agnostic in culture. Look, both your parents and mine chose the military as a profession. They've had to make compromises. Their battlefields were chosen for them. Same thing goes for Black guys like us. Others determine the battlefields upon which we have to survive. We just have to put the blade between our teeth, and crawl through the muck and shit in the jungle."

"Wait until Reed finds out that I'm doing this slavery project. What opinion would he have of me?"

"Forget about it. Though he impugns those who are profiting from slavery he's been cashing royalty checks from his Neo-Slave Narrative, *Flight to Canada*, for forty-five years. As for moving to Canada, I doubt that it'll ever happen. He's having too much fun complaining about how he's in exile and how it's easier to get a play done in Baden Baden or China or an op-ed published in Israel or Spain than in the United States and how the *London Overseas Book Review* has neglected his last five books. He complains about how critics want to keep Black culture locked in the '50s and '60s yet he's conducting a seminar at the California College of the Arts on James Baldwin, whose main influence was Henry James. When it comes to contradictions, the guy is the whole package. And he's still into this cross-cultural hybridization thing. He's overused the gumbo metaphor. Gumbo doesn't seem to be working for the Blacks in Berkeley and Oakland. Very few left since the last mayor invited in the Digitalites. They're overrunning the place. And other Colored groups seem to be faring better than the brothers and sisters. You go to the Kaiser pharmacy, on Broadway, Asians run it. You go to the Optometry or Ophthalmology departments. Same thing. The Kaiser restaurant, Hispanics run it. They call you 'boss' and 'captain,' like the Arabs. You go to the Berkeley Bowl, Hispanics and Asians again. You let China sink an American warship in the South China Sea and these crackers will round them up and haul them into internment camps like the Japanese. All of these people are getting paid for either masquerading as Blacks on behalf of people who've feared Blacks since before Puritan times or they're being used against Blacks and so I say to you Boa, go get paid. Everybody else is using slavery to make money, ain't no reason for you not to get paid as well."

Reed returned to the table, ponderously, and sat down. Took some deep breaths. He said, "Now Bowman, that's your name right, what are you up to these days?"

Boa started to talk about the lecture tour upon which he was about to embark but then instead said, "Oh, I'm trying to get by." Chappie smiled.

"Well. I got to get going." Reed picked up his iPhone, which he'd laid on the table. He went to the counter and ordered a double espresso to take out.

"The guy is a real character." Chappie said. When Reed returned to his home, he found that he'd left his phone on record after ending the interview with Chappie. He played the interview back and came to Chappie's comments about him while he was in Peet's restroom. Reed might be seen as an odd character, he was called "pathetic" by a Black slavery-minded rotund errand boy for the New York elite. A big-butt literary bounty hunter who gets an ice-cream-filled-chocolate doughnut every time he brings in a Negro's ear, figuratively. Reed might be bothered with knee pain, headaches, and neuropathy but on the page he expresses the wrath of an Old Testament god.

Chapter Six

THE FIRST DEBATE WAS to be held in New York.

He remembered seeing Shashi's photo in *The New York Observer* with the crowd of models and New York lit types

with whom he traveled. His photograph was a constant feature among Bill Cunningham's photographs in *The New York Times*. Boa flew to New York. As he was exiting from the plane he heard some laughter from some of the first-class passengers who were lined up. It was Shashi and his entourage, a bevy of lovely ladies, all but one wearing a sari. He noticed that the women were much darker than the men and one, who he found out later was Shashi's sister, Kala, was ink black. Purple lipstick. She was wearing a T-shirt and jeans. Dark glasses. Gucci. He walked ahead of the passengers who were leaving from coach. At the gate he caught up to Shashi. Boa introduced himself. *Wah uske kapade Macy's se kharidtaa hai*, Shashi thought. Boa stuck out his hand. Shashi looked at it in a contemptuous manner and moved on without saying anything. Before they disappeared into the terminal, he made a remark out of Boa's earshot. He gathered that it was at Boa's expense. Members of Shashi's entourage looked back at Boa and broke into laughter. While Shashi and his party were put up at the Hotel Pierre, Boa was installed at the Hotel Pennsylvania. After he checked in, unpacked, and took a shower, he took a walk around Seventh Avenue. Things had changed.

In 1968, well-dressed Blacks crowded Times Square. Some of them were attending a showing of *Rosemary's Baby*, the first of the demon child movies. Now, there were few Blacks in sight. Charles Blow had written that the police repression of Blacks, which had received the endorsement of the majority of White New Yorkers, had sent Blacks from New York into cities in New Jersey and elsewhere. High rents also played a role. Digitalites and Streamers had invaded Harlem. They wanted to rename it SoHa. Later, Boa rode in a taxi to a hall that had been rented on Central Park West for the first debate between Shashi Paramara and himself. As he mounted the steps of the building where the debate would take place, he noticed that some members of the audience had already arrived. Some were standing on the steps. Others were in the lobby. Purchasing liquor and coffee. He was greeted by his escort who showed him to his dressing room. It was a small room. A piano. No chair. A bowl full of pretzels. Two bottles of water. He was told that Shashi and his party had been provided with a suite on the top floor of the building. When it was minutes before the debate was to begin, the escort came and took him to the backstage area. The moderator, a tall blonde woman, came on stage and approached the center. The audience that had been chattering became quiet. "Ladies and Gentlemen, welcome to the third in a series of debates sponsored by the Hamilton Society, named for the great abolitionist and progressive, Alexander Hamilton. Tonight we are fortunate to have two well-known thinkers, Shashi Paramara." His introduction was accompanied by cheers and whistles. The applause lasted thirty seconds. "And his opponent." She paused. Looked at her notes. "I'm sorry— and William Bowman." "Peter," Bowman whispered to the moderator. There was silence. "Tonight's topic is 'Slavery. All that Bad?' Mr. Bowman's opinion will be that it was, as he put it, an abomination." This remark was followed by titters from the audience. "Mr. Paramara believes that slavery rescued Blacks from savagery." She nodded toward Shashi. He approached the lectern. The applause lasted for another minute. The audience was packed with representatives from right-wing think tanks.

"Ladies and Gentlemen, the playwright Jonathan Reynolds asked whether Blacks are better off now than they were in slavery. Good question. Under the guidance of merciful slave masters, the slaves contributed to the growth of the South so that it became one of the world's richest economies. Now you see their descendants pushing grocery carts through the cities. The only jobs available to them are in the recycling business. In the Inner City, nothing but carnage. The men spend their time idle and gathering on street corners. Their misogyny is used to control women who are given to loose sexual morality. They have become a burden on our country and are aggressively being replaced by hard-working immigrants. Scientists have proven that their low intelligence is preventing them from participating in the American Dream. Of course they are a very kinetic people. Quick hands and quick feet. They made our country proud when they brought gold medals home from the Olympics. Yet, when it comes to cerebral achievements, they are sorely lacking." Boa was writing furiously. He had to keep his hands busy, otherwise they would've been used to slug the bastard.

"But the slave masters found a way to channel their energy. This is why slavery should not be viewed as a horror but as a benevolent institution that gave the slaves something to do. Brought them from savagery to Christianity. And under civilized instruction there will come a time then their IQs are equal to ours." He sat down to vigorous applause.

The host person called on Boa. "Mr. Bowman." He was nervous. His legs felt weak. Of course, he'd done his Trotter/Wilson routine but this was the big league. The lights from chandeliers and cameras blinded him. He couldn't see the audience. He began haltingly but after a few minutes hit his stride. "Mr. Paramara has floated the usual misunderstandings about the slave trade. Two of our great classics, *Uncle Tom's Cabin* and *Huckleberry Finn*, show the horrors, in addition to the slave narratives written by the slaves themselves. Mrs. Stowe wrote about the breakup of families caused by the slave trade. Twain wrote about the hazards that beset the fugitive slave. Mr. Paramara is not aware of American history and as an assimilated Anglicized Indian is probably not even familiar with Indian history." That remark elicited boos and reminded Boa that Paramara was Columbia's star and the audience would be conservative. He continued politely pointing out some of the flaws in Paramara's arguments. At the end of the debate, there was applause. Boa approached Paramara to shake his hand. Paramara ignored him, even turned his back on Boa. Shashi approached the front of the stage, bent down, and greeted well-wishers and signed autographs. Paramara said something to his fans. Boa couldn't hear what he said. The fans looked toward Boa and began to laugh. It was obvious that Shashi had made some kind of remark that ridiculed Boa. As he was exiting from backstage, he ran into Jack Sharkey. Sharkey shook his hand. "Good job, Bowman. Firm but not angry. I think that we're going to have a great run with this show. Go a little easy on Shashi, though, that one slip about his being—how did you put it—Anglicized. You and I know that the guy is a wuss, but you don't have to say it. But you gotta give him credit. This guy can talk the hind legs off a donkey." On the plane returning to Oakland, he picked up a copy of *The New*

York Weekly Anglo. There was a story about the debate. Shashi's picture was prominent in the story. There were three paragraphs about his "brilliant" performance. The fact that Bowman was his debating partner came in the last sentence. "His opponent in the debate was Bowen (sic)."

Chapter Seven

THEIR TOUR CONTINUED. THE colleges, universities, libraries, and civic organizations would put Boa up in two-star motels, while Shashi and his entourage stayed in five-star hotels or the president's house. While poor students were being driven away from college as a result of high tuition costs, college presidents were living in palaces and being paid as much as Fortune Five Hundred CEOs. Sometimes they would have private dinners for Shashi and his party with a VIP list of guests without even inviting Boa. He'd order Chinese food or pizza from his hotel room. Their debates at colleges, on TV shows, and before civic organizations were going well. Shashi, of course, being a star, received generous applause, press coverage while Boa, during the question and answer period, was peppered with the toughest questions, some of them sarcastic and insulting. But at least he wasn't beaten up like the anti-slavery lecturers William Wells Brown or Frederick Douglass, or dragged off a train for demanding the same accommodations as the Whites, the way that Ida B. Wells was. The crowds would laugh at the insulting questions that the audience asked during the question and answer period and at Shashi's sarcastic rejoinders to his debating points. But this was better than teaching. You couldn't make a mistake in classrooms nowadays because the students were armed with all kinds of smart gadgets. Unlike the old days when appliances were mute, the new machines had an attitude and some were saying that it wouldn't be long before they would outthink us and maybe dominate us. Of course, given the mess that our species has made of the planet, could their rule be worse? According to *Wired*, January 27, 2016, "a computing system developed by Google researchers in Great Britain beat a top human player at the game of Go, the ancient Eastern contest of strategy and intuition that has bedeviled AI experts for decades."

During Boa's last year before he resigned from Woodrow Wilson, he'd attributed the authorship of *The Jungle* to Sinclair Lewis, instead of Upton Sinclair. He noticed two students laughing. They had consulted a smartphone, which corrected him. Being a public intellectual was different. You could shoot the breeze. Make generalizations, the intellectual equivalent of placing artificial flavoring and additives in food. All a public intellectual had to do was accost his opponent with a torrent of jargon. Interrupt a lot. Filibuster. Use words like "unpack." A lot of them had memorized the book, *More Word Power in 30 Days*. When you scrutinized their utterances, you'd find the content as lacking in nutrition as a croissant.

Chapter Eight

ONE DAY, HE RECEIVED an email from Sharkey. There had been a request from one of these posh San Francisco clubs that they have a debate. The sum of money was above that of their usual fee, which was quite nice. Of course, Shashi was paid maybe five times as much as Boa, but in comparison to the kind of money that he had been receiving from his lectureship at the community college, it was a princely sum.

Boa was one of these guys who had the television on around the clock. ESPN. SportsCenter. He got his news about the world from the BBC. He was keeping track of a story from India, once a trusted United States ally. A new Prime Minister was making bellicose sounds.

It started with a request from that Indian family that the Crown pay the descendants of those children who had been buggered by Lord Mountbatten. Part of their demand was the release of his private collection of child pornography as proof. Their lawyer's source was a book called *War of the Windsors*, and *The Sunday People* newspaper, which claimed that Lord Mountbatten was rumored to have been linked to the Kincora boys abuse network. "Lord Mountbatten, the last Viceroy in India, was renowned to be wildly promiscuous, bisexual, and to enjoy a bit of 'rough' or the pleasures of young working-class boys or indeed peasant Indian boys. In other words, Lord Mountbatten enjoyed rogering the children of lower classes and peasants," according to the paper.

The tensions between England and India, now heading toward number two after China as the leading world power, had escalated when the new premier, who was making an effort to unite India, Bangladesh, and Pakistan, a division that had been promoted by Winston Churchill, began to agree with the family that was suing the Crown. During a press conference he said, "Maybe there is something to Mountbatten's abusing Indian boys." The English ambassador to India protested, but the Indian Prime Minister, whose grandfather, an old diehard nationalist, gave him the name of Si after Siraj ud-Daulah, the last independent Nawab of Bengal, shrugged off the British protest. Siraj ud-Daulah gave the British all that they could handle until the conniving British picked a token to implement his downfall and murder. Upper-class Indian international partygoers, who called him Si, were shocked when Si entered politics. His wealthy parents were disappointed with Si, who had formerly been a playboy moving in a circle of Bollywood stars. Bollywood movies were even more down on Black people than Hollywood, which is saying something. Take the movie *Fashion*, the film starring Priyanka Chopra, who after a night of partying wakes up next to a Black man, which was to show that she had reached rock bottom. This movie was made by Madhur Bhandarkar, a Brahmin. In India, the film industry still does Blackface movies.

His friends spent a lot of time in night clubs, coffee shops, film festivals, London and Paris. But all of sudden Si had gotten the political bug and had worked his way up from a backbencher to Prime Minister.

Si fired back, calling the Prime Minister of England a *Bakri chod*, which, in Hindi, means "goatfucker." When word reached Downing Street, of the Indian Prime Minister's remark, the British Prime Minister became so angry that he threw a glass of wine against the wall. He had been preparing to toast the Russian ambassador, when an aide whispered the insult into his ear. To complicate the matter, some of the wine splashed on the Russian ambassador's coat. By the time RT got the news, the version had become that the British Prime Minister had splashed the wine into the visiting Russian ambassador's face. A Moscow newspaper called the British Prime Minister a "pedophile enabler." And said that "pedophilia among English men was an open secret." The American president supported the country's longtime partner by siding with the British Prime Minister and sent his ambassador to protest to India's ambassador to the United States.

One item captured Boa's attention. India's growth rate was projected to reach ten percent by 2025. By the end of the week, what had begun as an effort of an Indian family to right what they perceived as a wrong had escalated to threats. Military maneuvers. Si criticized the Irish for apologizing to the British for the murder of Lord Mountbatten. He said that they were insensitive to his criminal behavior when he was Indian Viceroy. Si alienated the Irish for calling the murder justifiable in light of Mountbatten's criminal behavior with Indian youngsters. The U.S. media, which was partially responsible for the invasion of Iraq, considered by some historians to be the worst U.S. foreign policy disaster, began depicting Si in a cartoonish fashion following the line of the administration. They used the phrases meant to demonize an opponent of the country. Si's mental capacity was questioned. India was called "a rogue nation." As usual, the media were serving as a stenographer for the government, as they do for the police.

Chapter Nine

THE NIGHT OF THE debate arrived. It was scheduled for eight o'clock and so Boa decided to take Bay Area Rapid Transit because it would take an hour or so if he were to drive. There was typically a bottleneck of traffic at the Bay Bridge toll plaza. When he arrived at the site of the debate he found one of those ornate neo-Classical buildings, which was constructed after the Earthquake of 1906. It was part of the City Beautiful movement, the intention of which was to recreate old 'Frisco as a second Paris. He almost expected Mark Antony to descend from the top of the stairs and deliver a soliloquy.

After climbing some marble steps, he arrived on the second floor of the space and was greeted politely by the hosts, who took him into the Green Room. Well, his Green Room. Shashi was such a star that his agent always requested that he have his own Green Room.

There was a pack of cokes, some nuts, and some oatmeal cookies laid out for Boa. Two apples. A bottle of water. About twenty minutes later, he heard some laughter and commotion in the Green Room adjoining his. He left his and entered Shashi's. Shashi was surrounded by some Indian beauties and a couple of blondes. His aides. He looked like one of these Bollywood stars. Dark glasses. Armani suit. Nails manicured. $500 haircut. There was a nice spread of food and drink for Shashi and his guests. He noticed something unusual. There was a small statue of a silver-faced woman. It was wearing peacock feathers, cowrie shells, and garland. It had been placed on the mantle above a fireplace which was white and elaborate. There appeared to be an offering placed before the statue.

Shashi gave Boa a slight but condescending smile. That was new. Waiters were passing out hors d'oeuvres and champagne. Someone came in and announced that they had fifteen minutes. He felt someone's eyes on him. He turned to see Kala on the other side of the room. She held a drink in her hand. Her informal wear was in contrast to the other Indian women in the room, who wore saris of intricate designs and elegant drapes. She was wearing a lavender-colored T-shirt. On the T-shirt appeared in black the words "*Bhaasha Svatantrata.*" The Black chauffeur, a tall skinny dude whom Columbia Speakers had hired to drive Shashi and his entourage around San Francisco approached him. He was enrolled at Laney College. Majoring in Political Science. Gauging Boa's fascination with the woman, he whispered into his ear: "You forget about that one, Kala— Shashi's younger sister. Calls English an imperialist language. Writes crazy articles demanding that only Hindi be spoken in India. She's the radical of the family and its darkest member. Besides, these Indians are very possessive with their women and aren't receptive to their dating outside of the group. Well, maybe White dudes are OK. They see marrying White guys as a way to improve their gene pool. But the brothers. Not. They will whip your ass if you try to date her."

"What do you mean, its darkest member?"

"Oh, you don't know? Indians can be as racist toward Black people as Whites. Some have called them the most racist people in the world. Not only do they hate Blacks but have problems with the darker members of their own families. You got mobs beating African students and a woman from Tanzania was stripped by a mob and marched through the streets." *A new bunch of racists coming into the country adding to the ones who are already here?* Boa thought. *African students and even diplomats having a hard time in India, especially in the rural areas? How could this be? This was the India that produced Gandhi. A Gandhi who inspired Martin Luther King, Jr. This Laney College student had to be exaggerating.*

"To Shashi and the men in his entourage of Brahmins, you're a Dalit."

"A what?"

"A Dalit. An Untouchable."

"That's ridiculous. India is a democracy. Gandhi, one of the greatest men in history, who ranks with Buddha and Christ, influenced Dr. King and his philosophy of Nonviolence." He walked away from the young man. And began to mingle.

He looked across the room. She was still staring at him, but when she saw him returning her look, she averted her eyes. Catching this exchange, the chauffeur, picking a hors d'oeuvre from a waiter who was passing them out said, sighing: "OK. Don't say I didn't warn you. You don't have to believe me. You should read Dr. B. R. Ambedkar. The Hindus just about invented racism. The South is a racial utopia in comparison to the way Blacks are treated in India."

"Young man. Like many of your age group, you're given to wild conspiracy theories." Boa walked away. The South a racial utopia. These young Black and Brown Millennials were innocent. For Boa and his generation the South would never be a racial utopia. Sterling Brown was right in his poem. The South would always be hell.

They took their positions on stage. Shashi received the usual healthy round of applause, while there were a smattering of boos that greeted Boa. They engaged in the usual back and forth until it came to Shashi's rebuttal.

"One has to agree with that giant intellect William Kristol, who urged us to respect Robert E. Lee and Jonathan Zimmerman of New York University, who said that the Confederate soldiers should be revered for 'laying down their lives for their countrymen,'" began Shashi. Boa leaped to his feet. He had been advised by Sharkey to be reasonable but he was getting weary of Shashi's offensive remarks about the brothers and sisters. "The same can be said of the Nazi generals and soldiers who committed atrocities, that they laid down—" he began to say. But before he could continue the moderator said that they'd run out of time. This was accompanied by a sneer at Boa.

"But, I was just beginning my rebuttal," Boa protested. The moderator, a White man, began praising Shashi. All about his cogent arguments as opposed to Boa's "incoherent, primitive ones." He added, "When you make analogies to the Nazis you always lose." The moderator summarized the debate. He said that Shashi's brilliant arguments concluded that the North had it wrong when it invaded the South, which had shown the folly of liberating men and women who were adult children and needed kindly management. Nodding to Shashi's billionaire producer seated in the front row, the moderator said, "We hope that your musical, *Robert E. Lee, The General Who Rocked*, will be a great success." Shashi's benefactor was a slumped-over bald man who was leaning on a cane. He was sitting next to a blonde who was wearing a mink coat and expensive jewelry. She was heavily made up and wearing a slinky red dress. Yves, Baldwin's character in *Another Country*, would have a field day with this woman. Obviously a Republican. He was her sugar daddy. Her lipstick had been applied thickly. One of Carl Sandburg's "painted women." She was chewing gum. Noticing Boa's staring at her, she removed the gum and stuck it underneath her seat. The moderator, turning his back to Boa, was about to rise and shake Shashi's hand to the thunderous applause of the audience when a man rushed on stage and whispered into the ear of the moderator. The moderator frowned. He turned, his face red as a Mexican red pepper. He rose from his chair. "Ladies and Gentlemen, India just shot down an American passenger plane." Screams of horror went up from the audience. The moderator glared at Shashi. Those who a moment before were nodding their heads to Shashi's points about slavery were now shouting at him. "Get that Indian nigger," somebody yelled. One of the audience members reached the stage and began pummeling Shashi. Boa tried to protect him, but was punched and landed on the floor. Security rescued Shashi and hurried him and his entourage from the stage and, once outside, pushed them into waiting limousines, which sped off. The hall was left a mess. Overturned chairs. The floor slippery from drinks that had been spilled. Clothing left on the floor and coats left in the cloak-room because their owners had rushed from the audience to the stage, from where they chased Shashi and his party out of the building. He walked outside of the lecture hall and found himself standing alone on Van Ness Avenue.

A Harley Davidson pulled up. It was Shashi's sister. With her attire, black leather jacket, jeans, helmet, her American appearance had come in handy. "Get on," she said. He got on the back and held her around the waist. He gave her directions to his home located near Children's Hospital in Oakland, which began in the stables of a mansion owned by Solomon E. Alden, a former squatter who was part of the land theft of property belonging to the Peralta family. His son-in-law, John Edgar McElrath, was a major in the Confederate army. She just about flew across the Bay Bridge, weaving in and out of traffic. She was going so fast that from time to time he was tempted to ask her to let him off. When they arrived at his home he invited her inside for coffee, but she said that she had to get home. She was living in a home located in the Berkeley Hills. Later he found that she was the guest of a Black woman who had written a bestselling memoir entitled *My Triple Oppression*. With the millions from her book sales, she had bought an elaborate estate which was the former home of a Funk star. She had been Kala's guest when attending a writers' conference in Mumbai.

Before she started her drive to the Hills, he asked her, "The mob went after your brother and his entourage. How did they miss you?"

"White Americans are always mixing me up with a Black person. Being Black doesn't work in my country. Over here, it comes in handy sometimes." *What? Black coming in handy. In the United States?* Boa thought.

She didn't have to worry about members of a mob showing their faces up there in the Berkeley Hills. Once inside his home, he turned on the local news. Some of the local citizens, who were asked to respond to the downed plane, urged the Governor of California to intern the Indian population. Hysteria promoted by talk shows led some of the White callers to demand the deportation of Indian citizens, even those who had lived in the States for generations. He checked his email. Out of curiosity, he googled the name of Shashi's sister. She was a professor of Postcolonial Studies at an Indian University. There was a photo of her and other students confronting the police. A campus demonstration. They were carrying signs that read *"Bhaasha Svatantrata."* She was on sabbatical, which explained her presence in the United States. But Boa had problems with her hypothesis. That English was the language of Imperialism. Our English!! Boa thought. The English that accommodated outsiders? The language that paid the rent. The language of the people. While the court spoke Latin, the people spoke English. A big tent language, which included both pagan and Christian influences. That welcomed Shakespeare's iambic pentameter as well as the hip-hopper Rick Ross's octameter in his song "Work." *They askin' questions and I heard they even lookin' for me / Ridin' up and down the block, they showin' pictures of me.* English accommodates King Alfred as well as Iceberg Slim. Alurista as well as Ishmael Hope. Professor Tracey's Irish Green English and the Hispanic Brown English and Toni Cade Bambara's Black English. Jane Austen's High English and Marlon James's Reggae English. A language that began with chaos over time had settled into a word order: adjectives, nouns, prepositions, objects direct and indirect. Niger-Congo languages were also SVO.

Hindi was an SOV language. A language that placed the verb at the end. For example, I read a book every day, becomes *I, every day, a book read. Main roz ek kitab padhta hoon.* But then languages that placed the action words at the end might be ones with the deeper wisdom than those that placed the verbs at the beginning, like shooting from the hip instead of contemplating an action before committing oneself to it. Yoruba, an African language, dropped verbs. *Won buru* = They bad.

Yet English was a language that could even be appreciated by the illiterate, as singers performing in English entertained those who could not read. A language of imperialism? A language whose syntax was flexible while that of some other languages was fixed. My English. The language of the Wobblies and Harriet Tubman. But also the language that gave us the construction "Greed is Good." Traveling with Shashi and his entourage stirred his interest in Bharat. Its history. Its people. Its language.

He signed up for online lessons. Maybe he needed a vacation from English. Maybe it's unhealthy for one language to have a patent on one's brain. Chappie had said that his learning Japanese allowed him to see American society from inside and out. Maybe playing around with language would re-energize his brain. Zhou Youguang, known as the father of Pinyin for creating the system of Romanized Chinese writing, lived until he was 111. Stephen Hawking had said that the brain was a muscle. Learning a language might be considered mental push-ups.

He learned that the religious origin of Hindi occurred around 8–9 AD. That it advanced in the works of writers like the Jain poet Vidyapati, whose book Boa purchased. On January 26, 1950, Hindi became the Official Language of the Republic of India, but younger people, in order to get jobs, were abandoning Hindi for English. In the beginning of his lessons, he learned to say *"Hindi mein ustāad Hona tahakhānā mein bait kar sharab pina kē jaisā nahii haiy.*" No it was difficult. With Japanese and Yoruba, you were aided by dictionaries when seeking nouns, verbs, adjectives and pronouns and prepositions. For Hindi, some had definitions and some didn't. In Hindi you flitted from dictionary to dictionary. There was no standardized spelling. Some of the words for which you were searching could be found in songs rather than in dictionaries.

And when words were not found you were directed to forums about words that went on for a number of pages. Moreover some words originated from Urdu, Arabic, or Persian. You become grateful that you have simple English regardless of the gobble-dygook one finds in the grammar books. No wonder Hindi has some relationship to the *Kama Sutra*. In its complexity. English prefers the missionary position. With this SOV language Boa had to rearrange the wiring in his brain that was used to the English syntax.

Why was any information about Bharat missing from the schools that he attended? Except for its soccer teams, Boa knew little about *Bharata ke Itihaas*. At the Davy Crockett Elementary School that he attended while his parents were stationed in Texas (there was a big old statue of Crockett in a coonskin cap located in the front of the school), he and other students were taught that all of the earth's knowledge was located in a few European countries. However, Cervantes, the father of the English novel, was inspired by a Muslim storyteller. Boa and his fellow students were taught that the White man was a little lower than the angels. That there were savages in Africa who would eat you. That people in India sat around all day wooing cobras from baskets, and in the movies there was Sabu the Elephant Boy. Boa was no Indian specialist but he knew that Asia, Africa, and India had literary and oral traditions in storytelling reaching back thousands of years. He had learned in school that English was a member of the Indo-European category of languages and indeed there were German and therefore English words that were derived from Sanskrit. But none of his teachers would explain the Indo part. When the pundits (a Sanskrit word) spoke of "The West," they were often using words that were derived from a language created in India, but India, in their minds, had nothing to do with The West? Why didn't they place pictures of Black and Brown people in books as to better explain what Indo-European meant? Why didn't they list some of the words that we use in everyday life, words that didn't originate in England and France, which is what members of the overseas Intellectual, Artistic elites mean when they refer to Europe, but originated in Sanskrit. Words like Aryan, Avatar, Bandana, Buddha, Candy, Cheetah, Cowrie, Crimson, Crocus, Dharma, Dinghy, Ganja, Guru, Jackal, Juggernaut, Jungle, Jute, Karma, Lacquer, Lilac, Loot, Maharajah, Mahatma, Mandala, Mandarin, Mantra, Mugger, Musk, Nark, Nirvana, Opal, Orange, Panther, Punch, Pundit, Sandal, Sapphire, Sari, Shaman, Shampoo, Shawl, Singapore, Sulfur, Sugar, Swami, Swastika, Thug, Yoga, Yogi.

Is this why White nationalists prefer the incongruous combination of Judeo-Christian (which might include Ethiopians!) to Indo-European because such a hyphenated expression suggests that White civilization might be tainted with Brownness/Blackness? The Indo-European culture is more prevalent in everyday life—it involves how we communicate with each other—than Judeo-Christian culture, which has a following that is dwindling. Moreover, though the term "Judeo-Christian" was used by right wingers, there was evidence that the phrase offended some. Commenting on the use of the term by far-Right Senator Ted Cruz, Salomon Gruenwald, a rabbi in Denver, Colorado, addressed Cruz in the *Forward*:

> *You claim to love and support the state of Israel and, as with "Judeo-Christian," you invoke your love of Israel to bolster your bellicose foreign policy. You recently invited the endorsement of Pastor Mike Bickle of*

the International House of Prayer. Bickle, like many evangelical Christian Zionists, believes we are living in the "end times" and that Jesus will return any day now to take up good Christians in the Rapture, leaving the rest of us to languish in a millennium-long war whose battlefield will be the land of Israel. Bickle, among other meshugas (that's Jewish for "crazy-talk"), teaches that Hitler was a "hunter" sent by God to drive the Jewish people to resettle Israel, thereby hastening the battle of Armageddon. Senator Cruz, if you want to promote your agenda and claim it is a reflection of your religious values, go right ahead—but don't exploit my religion and my people to do it.

Were there alternatives to newsman Sam Donaldson's view of North America? That it was a sea of Judeo-Christian Whiteness in which Blacks had best learn to swim. For his survival, Boa and Black members of his class had learned to swim. Not only swim but do backstrokes and flips. Sometimes he was over his head in deep water, as when he unintentionally began trouble for his school because of his lecture about Trotter. He was being blamed for igniting the students' desire to take down the statue of Wilson, Klan admirer. The scourge of Haiti. This caused a lot of resentment from his colleagues, but before there could be retaliation—for the remarks about the Monroe Trotter / Woodrow Wilson feud—he had been pole-vaulted from the dreary life of teaching at a community college to a star on the lecture circuit. Conjugating Hindi, getting used to a word order that placed the verb at the end, was a struggle for Boa, but when it came to the present continuous, Boa was like Stephen Curry, knocking down three-pointers from the entrance of the Oracle Arena.

Chapter Ten

BOA SHOWED UP AT the Oakland Federal Building at eight a.m. Carried a box that contained receipts, cancelled checks, bills, travel expenses, etc. After he passed through security he took the elevator to the floor where the audit would be conducted. They put him in a room where he sat until an agent lumbered into the room and introduced himself. He was a stocky Black man with a bumpy face. A sagging chin. Looked to be about forty-five. His sleeves were rolled up. He wore a white shirt and plain tie. He shook hands with Boa and slowly took the seat across from him. He began studying the material that Boa had brought. He'd look at some paper and then look up at Boa. Finally, he said:

"The trips. That's why you were flagged. Why so much travel and why do you think that you can get a write-off?"

"Those trips are in connection with my profession."

"And what is that?"

"I am a lecturer and recently I have been traveling the country under the auspices of the Columbia Speakers Bureau."

The agent eyed him suspiciously. "What did you lecture about?"

His response was friendly. "I talk about the conflict between Monroe Trotter and Woodrow Wilson, who was president of the United States." The interviewer paused. Stroked his chin. Repeated the gesture. Finally he frowned.

"Now I recognize you. You're the guy who told those students to skip school and hang around in downtown Oakland."

"They were practicing their right to Civil Disobedience."

"Civil Disobedience? They were just using their Civil Disobedience to goof off downtown and trash the taxpayers' property."

"Those were just a few kids who got out of hand."

"Well, in my day, we cracked the books and not the windows of small businesses. I don't know where guys like you get off. Instead of instilling Christian values, you're putting them up to mischief. It's because of you that a lot of these teenage girls are getting pregnant. You're also probably responsible for the Oakland Raiders moving to Las Vegas. And you got the nerve to show up here wearing a Warriors' T-shirt. They need a place that's more tranquil than Oakland, where if it ain't the students tearing up downtown, it's these suburban kids—these anarchists coming in from out of town."

"What? You're joking. And why is a representative of the federal government telling me about Christian values?"

"The last regime did it to us. We're in charge now and so guys like you had better watch out. You'll be hearing from us soon about your deductions." With that he got out of the chair, picked up the box of receipts and cancelled checks all the while glaring at Boa, and left the room.

His pronouncement of deductions had the sound of a snarl. Boa figured that he was going to be $60,000 shorter. When he left the federal building after trying to justify the reasons behind his deductions it was time for lunch. So Boa went to Mexicali Rose on Eighth Street for a take-out burrito. When the burrito was prepared, he left the restaurant. Across the street was the police station. A police horse was standing there. He had to walk by the station in order to reach his car because Mexicali Rose's parking lot was full. Mexicali was one of the places in Oakland where Black diners felt comfortable, racial profiling having become intense, not only in the Über restaurants but those managed by Chinese and Koreans. As he walked past the horse it said, "You crazy. You blew your cover and now

Brigitte is going to be on your ass like a horsefly on shit." Boa turned around. The horse was just standing there. An auditory hallucination?

PART TWO

Chapter Eleven

AFTER BREAKFAST, BOA WENT to the front window. The Übers, who had taken over a home where a Black family had lived for decades, had left their old nasty yellow truck in front of his house, as well as their outdoor privy for use of the workers. This seemed odd because there was tons of space in front of the house that they were flipping. The flipper's method was to pay the Black family peanuts for selling the house and then bring in cheap labor to renovate the place. The buyers got a cheap Chinese-speaking crew, and after they finished, they sold it four times the price of their purchase. Another way that the Übers used to intimidate was to load up your lawn with dog shit. Boa wasn't the only resident of a neighborhood undergoing Überization who was bothered by this particular habit of the Übers.

Economist Julianne Malveaux wrote:

> *I hate these entitled white folks who leave their dog poop everywhere but in their own garbage cans and have the nerve to say it is "too much" for them to have to carry the poop home. And I especially hate, a strong but real word, the dog owners who don't think their dogs need to be leashed 'cause their dogs (but not me) need to be free to roll up on me, sniff on me, despite the fact that I do not like (and am, in fact, somewhat petrified by) large dogs. The level of angst that I experience varies, but some days it leads to near apoplexy.*

The Indian crisis was the first headline in the morning news. Boa was watching from the tub. He'd installed a TV on a bathroom wall. Buses containing Indians from Silicon Valley were seen speeding toward San Jose airport on the roads lined with Americans. They were throwing garbage at the buses and shouting racist insults. Not only were the protestors White. They were Black and Hispanic as well. Some were waving flags and shouting "U.S.A! U.S.A!" Others were waving Confederate flags, symbol of the invisible Empire, which with a recent election wasn't so invisible anymore as they were a few steps from the Oval Office. Indians who wore their traditional clothing were being dragged off Bay Area Rapid Transit. Hoping that floating a new enemy might improve its ratings, Cable TV was looping the same footage of American bodies being retrieved from the wreckage of the plane that was said to have been shot down under the orders of Si. Twenty-four hours per day. Crawlers all day. People who'd never been to India were presented on panels as India experts.

Chapter Twelve

THERE WAS A KNOCK at the door. It was Shashi. He was disguised. Hoodie. Dark glasses. He'd applied some skin darkener. Boa acted cool. Pretended that he didn't recognize him. "Yes?" Boa asked.

Shashi was wearing the kind of shoes that LeBron advertises. But Boa, who had become familiar with his body language, recognized him at once. After all of the ugly things that he had said about hip-hoppers, here he was dressed like one. Underwear showing. Seems an angry mob had surrounded the Mark Hopkins Hotel, where he and his party were staying. Shashi had escaped through the kitchen. "Hey, Boa, don't you recognize me. It's Shashi. Your debating partner. How do you like my disguise?"

"What can I do for you, Shashi?"

"I need a place to stay, old man. This unrefined throng accosted me. It was absolutely beastly." He always talked like an upper-middle-class Victorian character from Galsworthy's *The Forsyte Saga*. Writer C. J. Wallia gave a reason for this. He said that while Oxford was teaching the Latin and Greek classics, they consigned nineteenth-century English novelists for instruction in the colonies. He was trembling. His eyes were red, an indication that he hadn't slept well. He kept looking up and down the street.

"It would be only a short time. My friends are attempting to get me to Mexico. From there I can fly home." Home? After all the ratty things he had said about India. Writing those fucking articles about how he viewed himself as a "mid-Atlantic man" in those fucking hi-ass New York and Washington magazines. He said that he had found out that he was a mid-Atlantic man by consulting his "psychic database." Wrote a piece in the *London Overseas Book Review* about how Maya Angelou had spoken of Shakespeare as a universal author, as though Blacks had said that he wasn't. A Strawman. He was giving a literary schoolboy's apple to the guardians of White Supremacy. He was scoring brownie points for his puppet masters, using the late author as a lance against those who opposed the colonial curriculum. It figures. Picking a fight with Blacks was almost an initiation rite for those American-born children of immigrants. The ones who desired to assimilate into Whiteness. Which meant that you were opposed to diversity, which had become an uncomfortable prospect for some Whites, even the academic class, who were not intellectually curious and wanted those who were not like them to make things comfortable for them. Shashi had begun his career by interning for a magazine founded by an Irish American, who perfected the art of creating an intellectual brawl with Blacks. The right was packed with Irish Catholics like him. They wanted so hard to be accepted by the Anglos. This Irish Catholic founder even took up the harpsichord and played Handel he was so horny about pleasing his Anglo backers. Lecturing Blacks about their morals. Yet, when the founding editor visited his right-wing buddies at Dartmouth, he would get so drunk that he'd piss in the bathroom sink.

He sued a critic who called him a "Nazi." The judge awarded him one dollar. Another writer, a member of the East Coast punditry elite, had scolded Black Americans. Said that they should adopt bourgeois values. He was found out to be doing two grams of coke per day.

Missing from Shashi's list were Hindi classics, which Boa was beginning to purchase online. But of course, Shashi was the one who said that as long as millions of Indians spoke Hindi instead of English, India would be barred from entering the twenty-first century. He considered it a dead language of no use in the modern world. He'd said that India was also being held back by its polytheistic obsessions. Like the rites held for Kali, the goddess of death and destruction. All of the "dark superstitions" surrounding this goddess. Mothers warning their children against stepping over broken eggs, entrails of animals. Abstaining from eating brains, livers, or hearts. They even had a goddess of wheat. You get on the bus in India and you see the passengers fiddling with their lucky charms. Shashi said that millions of Indians, like their counterparts in Africa, even the PhDs among them, still believed in witches. He then got on the Indians about their cow thing. Cow dung was even used in sacred ceremonies. Shashi pointed out that 32.6 billion tons of carbon dioxide or 51 percent of annual worldwide GHG emissions were traceable to cows, pigs, and other farm animals. The future of the globe was held in hostage. All because of stupid superstition. "I think that we can work something out, Shashi. Follow me."

He took Shashi into his large basement. Installed there was a bath, shower, bed, and small refrigerator. Shashi looked around. *Yeh vaisey shaandar nivas nahi hai(n) ki jiskaa main aadi hoon, phir bhi abhi key liye chal jaaye(n)gaa*, Shashi thought. He would be comfortable. Momentarily, Shashi was sound asleep. It had been a rough twenty-four hours for Shashi. He slept until the next day. Without removing his clothes. The next morning, there was a knocking at the door. One of those NextDoor.com angry Übers stood before him. His face was contorted. He had a wild look. Like a movie savage. He was surrounded by some other Übers all armed with pit bulls with which they intimidated their Black neighbors.

"You see an Indian come this way?"

Mobs were roaming the country looking for Indians. The media, as usual, was egging them on to harm this latest object of hate, following the lead of their fear-mongering ancestors, the colonial press, a sure way to boost ratings, instill panic, and sell products.

"No. And I've been here for the last three hours."

The man wasn't convinced. He looked at Boa skeptically. Looked over Boa's shoulder and into the house. The mob moved on toward Fifty-second Street and Market. He turned on the TV.

The Pentagon announced that the fleet was heading toward the Indian Ocean and that the government was considering internment camps for Indian American citizens. For their own safety. Mobs in New York were trashing Indian restaurants.

Prime Minister Si accepted no blame for the downing of the aircraft. Said that India had nothing to do with it. The American media and politicians called him a liar and some in Congress requested sanctions against India.

Chapter Thirteen

BOA WALKED TO AN Arab-owned store on Market and Forty-fourth to buy some goods. It was disguised as a grocery store whose real profits were made by selling liquor to the poor, those who remained in a neighborhood that was becoming more and more techie. It was like a liquor museum, an encyclopedic list of brands that you'd think were discontinued filled the shelves. In the rear was a cafeteria where South Asians could purchase their favorite ethnic foods. They wore T-shirts and baseball caps that read, "I am not Indian." There was a list of the lunch menu items written on a blackboard suspended from a wall. The Arabs had placed a heavy-set-looking Black clerk named Lanie up front so that if someone wanted to rob the place, he'd be the first that they'd shoot. Boa bought some cream cheese, crackers, yogurt, nuts, peanut butter, half a dozen bottles of Kombucha, twelve cans of sardines. He bought some tomatoes, lettuce, brussels sprouts. He bought a take-out plate of vegetable biryani for Shashi. A couple of samosas. Some pieces of naan. Lanie was always giving Boa a hard time. Perhaps because he was so full of self-loathing that he hated those who shared his skin color. He was black as the black on the keys of a Mac Pro. Boa was next in line. Lanie was arguing with one of those customers who was kind of lit up. "Why can't I have credit Motherfucker? You got an ass like a water buffalo. Matter of fact I came into the store the other day and he was talking to his ass." The Arabs broke up with laughter, which encouraged the man to hurl more insults at Lanie. The Arab manager told Lanie to give him some credit for the pint of whiskey that the customer desired.

"But he already is behind two months," Lanie pleaded, in a high-pitched voice.

"You going to pay me when you get your SSI, boss?" the Arab asked.

"Man you know I'm good for it." The Arab nodded his head toward Lanie, who was fuming. The man just about did a little jig. Poor people, some of whom were receiving credit from the Arab store owner, often provided the store owner with demeaning, self-deprecating entertainment. The poor women, sex. Scowling, Lanie put the customer's pint of Hennessy into a bag and the customer reeled away. Clutched his pint and just about skipped out of the store after giving the Arab a fist bump. As for his part, the store owner, when dealing with the poor Blacks who lived in a couple of run-down hotels nearby, sprinkled his vocabulary with some Ebonics. Often it was dated. He'd say something like "Hey, brother man. What's shakin' with the bakin'?" or a variation. His calling his Black customers "boss" or "captain" was meant to be ironic? Boa approached the counter. Lanie ignored him. He even came out from behind the counter and began packing some products on a shelf. When he finished, he returned to behind the counter to ring up Boa's purchases. After packing them he asked rudely. "Is that all?" Boa shook his head.

"Wait a minute."

"Yes?"

"What you doing buying Mediterranean food for? You don't usually buy no Mediterranean food."

The media, in order to whip up ratings, had warned citizens to be on the lookout for Americans who changed their dietary habits. Like all of a sudden buying Mediterranean food. They might be harboring Indians. He was looking at Boa as though he wanted to fight. In fact, he had his fists balled.

"Oh. Thought I'd change my diet. Try something new."

Lanie packed the take-outs and other items rudely and pushed the bag toward Boa.

Chapter Fourteen

IN A LARGE ROOM located at NATO headquarters, the movements of Si, the Indian Prime Minister, were being watched on a big screen. Visiting Sivaganga, he laid a wreath at the memorial for freedom fighter Velu Nachiyar, the queen who fought against the British. Next he was off to China. He visited the Terracotta Army Museum, the Daqingshan Buddhist temple, where thirteen centuries ago monks from India translated scriptures into Chinese. The next day it was announced that China and India would engage in naval exercises in the Indian Ocean. Next, Si was off to a Moscow meeting with Russia's Prime Minister, who was ridiculed behind his back by his guards as "little Czar," as a result of his being born with micro genitals. Atrazine had been used on the farm where he grew up. This explained why he was always showing his steroids-loaded body to the cameras. Posing half nude on a horse. Or shown wrestling some other beefed-up opponents, who knew better than to win. Si was capitalizing on what was perceived as an insult to the Russian ambassador by reminding Russia of its Asian heritage and calling for a Pan Asian response to the war overtures being made by the United States and Britain. Watching the whole thing on a video screen inside NATO headquarters, sitting alone at the head of the table with her boots on the table was Boa's mother, General Bowman.

Chapter Fifteen

ONE MORNING, SHASHI RISKED being detected by coming to the first floor. Boa was watching TV. Some Indians were trying to enter Toronto. The people in Canadian Customs said that they'd already had enough Indians and because of the crisis with the United States and England, their allies, had enough trouble keeping an eye on those already in the country.

What was becoming an underground railroad for Indians, constructed by those who were sympathetic to their cause, had resulted in problems for some of their protectors. After public demand pressured Congress into constructing internment camps, those who were caught sheltering Indians would be arrested. The Fugitive Indian Law was being debated in Congress. In one case, thirty or so Indians got into a brawl. The light-skinned ones who claimed to be descendants of Aryans wanted to be separated from the darker ones, called Dravidians. They wanted their host to put up a partition in the basement where he was hiding them. Their bickering had spilled out from their hiding place into the streets and their benefactor had been arrested along with them. These light-skinned Indians who viewed themselves at the top of the phony caste system had risked their safety and that of those they regarded as "Untouchables." Boa noticed Shashi standing at the top of the basement stairs. "What? Shashi, you're really pushing it. Suppose somebody saw you."

"I was getting claustrophobic down there, my dear fellow. I just wanted to thank you for taking me in, old man. I will always be indebted to you. After that insufferable rabble accosted me, I had nowhere to turn. What can I do for you?"

Oh, Boa's ghetto side thought: *Now that the White man is closing in on your ass, you humble,* dropping his verb, a Yoruba retention. As hard as he tried, Boa failed to silence his ghetto thoughts that arose from time to time. Maybe one day there would be medication for it. Preferably over the counter. Shashi pulled up a chair at the kitchen table while Boa looked outside to check to see whether the coast was clear. Satisfied, he joined Shashi at the table. He thought how proud the generation of Black leaders who were born around 1900 would be of him. Those who believed that there should be solidarity between American Blacks and the Asiatic Black man. Those leaders of the early twentieth century, including the honorable Elijah Muhammad, didn't know how close to the truth they were. The *India Times* study offered:

> *Migratory route of Africans: Between 135,000 and 75,000 years ago, the East-African droughts shrunk the water volume of Lake Malawi by at least 95%, causing migration out of Africa. Which route did they take? Researchers say their study of the tribes of Andaman and Nicobar islands using complete mitochondrial DNA sequences and its comparison [to] those of world populations has led to the theory of a "southern coastal route" of migration from East Africa through India. This finding is against the prevailing view of a northern route of migration via Middle East, Europe, south-east Asia, Australia and then to India . . .*

"You called yourself a mid-Atlantic man, which caused you to be embraced by the country's cultural elite, but as in the past, when a country becomes an adversary of the United States—for those whose ancestry can be traced to the enemy country—all bets are off. This is what happened to Japanese, German, and Italian Americans."

"You have a point. Ever since the government classified me as a fugitive, my bank account has been frozen and so I don't have access to the $150,000 that the investors deposited for the rights to my musical about Robert E. Lee. I've called my friends who made me president of PEN New York for financial help. None of them would return my calls. None of them would take me in."

"You what?"

"I said—" Boa grabbed his smart phone.

"What are you doing, old chap?"

"Look. It's bad enough that I do your laundry and buy you food, which puts me in jeopardy, but if they find out that I am sheltering you, I could be charged under the proposed Fugitive Indian Law."

Yeh Biryani kharaab haiy, Shashi thought.

"Hand over that phone. I'll keep it until you get transportation to Mexico. Besides, the only reason that PEN New York made you president was because they didn't want to deal with traditional African Americans who are on to their liberal bullshit and most likely to call them on it. That's the same reason that they're pushing these African writers. They're being brought in as cultural reinforcement by these wannabe colonialists. Their role is to undermine the Black vernacular, a language of uprising, and Britishfy the Black writing scene. Moreover, Western intellectuals have always had this thing about India. Look at this Yoga craze. The average Indian living in India can't afford no Yoga. The Western intellectuals' fascination with India began with their problems with Judeo-Christian thought. Of course, they went overboard. Kant even said that the origin of mankind was in Tibet. It wasn't long before—" Weary of the rant, Shashi interrupted Boa.

"I'm sorry old chap. How can I ever repay you?"

Boa paused for a moment. "I'm treated like shit when we debate. You get the press. You get the VIP suites. You get the fly babes. You get the private dinners. You can pay me back by getting that Columbia Speakers Bureau to give me the same accommodations as you."

"But I'm the star The people pay to see me."

"OK," Boa said removing his smart phone and beginning to dial Homeland Security, "I'll bet the government would like to know your whereabouts."

"OK. OK. We both will be treated equally. I'll talk to the Bureau."

Chapter Sixteen

IT WAS SHASHI'S BIRTHDAY. Boa discovered this by reading Wikipedia. He thought that he would surprise him. Soma was a drink that was mentioned in some of the ancient texts that he was reading. So he went up to the Arab mom and pop store, and bought a bottle. It was a kind of brandy. Lanie eyed him as he placed the bottle into a bag.

"What kind of drink is this? We don't get many requests for it. In fact, I don't remember none. What you doing buying it for?"

"Just wanted to give it as a gift." As he walked out of the store, he felt Lanie's angry glare at his back.

When he entered the basement, Shashi was taking a bath. He put the bottle of Soma on the table. He noticed a manuscript that was lying on the table. It was the book for the musical *Robert E. Lee, The General Who Rocked*. Boa began to read it. The more pages he read the angrier he got. He started making notes. When Shashi emerged from the bath, he found Boa shaking his head. He had doused himself with some kind of perfume. It stank up the room. Like Boa, Shashi had an athlete's body. Like the kind advertised by GMC.

"What's wrong?" Shashi asked Boa as he placed the manuscript back on the table. "Nothing," Boa mumbled. He poured the brandy into two brandy glasses that he'd bought at Bed Bath & Beyond in Jack London Square. Shashi smiled. "How were you able to find this? Delightful. I'm touched." He placed the glass to his nose and started to comment on its bouquet and aroma, whatever.

"A toast. *Janamdin Kee Shubhaechaen*, Shashi!" Boa really messed up the pronunciation, but Shashi was so touched that he ignored it. That morning he had greeted him in Hindi. *Suprabhaat* for good morning. He'd conveyed his annoyance at being greeted in Hindi, which, for him, was such a backward language, but since it was his birthday, he didn't mind.

"Why, thank you, Boa, it's okay that you use Hindi on this special occasion, but I wish that you would refrain from using it in the future."

"Thought that you needed something to cheer you up on your birthday. And I wanted also to acknowledge the fact that after hearing that your sister was in some kind of movement that opposed English as an imperialist language, I began reading 'Hindi in 7 Days,' something I downloaded from the Internet."

Shashi began to laugh. "Why would you want to learn Hindi? It's of no practical use in these modern times. When my father died, it was the end of the use of Hindi in my household. Most of my sisters and brothers, who were educated in London, marked that as a welcomed break with the past. All except for my sister Kala. She got mixed up with some of these bloody Hindu nationalists at the university. Went around criticizing instructors who taught in English. Indian writers who wrote in English. She's been nothing but trouble for my family. An embarrassment. We've always had to protect her from those who resent her dark skin. She's as black as Newgate's knocker."

Shashi put on a kimono that Boa had lent him. They sat for about forty-five minutes. Refilling each other's drinks while listening to Ravi Shankar. After about five drinks, Boa got what was bothering him off his chest.

"I glanced at your script," his eyes on the manuscript that lay on the table.

"Oh. What do you think?"

"You have Martha Washington's granddaughter, Mary Custis Lee, helping out the slaves?"

He began to read.

Act 3, Scene 5
Night. The lovely dark-haired and aristocratic
Mary Custis Lee steals away from the main house
at Arlington and heads toward the slave cabins. She
knocks on the cabin door of Old Nurse.

Old Nurse: Missy Lee. What is you doin down
here this time of the night? Here let me put one
of these blankets over your delicate alabaster
frame.

(With a wave of a delicate hand Mary Custis Lee
refuses the offer. The absolutely beautiful Mary
Custis Lee places a basket on a table. She draws
back the covers. Old Nurse as a child ran to the
gates and opened them so that her master President
George Washington could ride through; she then ran
all over the plantation shouting "Massa Washington
home, Massa Washington home." Whereupon all the
slaves would stop their tasks and walk toward the
General belting out one of them good old spirituals.
Old Nurse smiles as she sees jars of peanut butter,
jam, a ham, a chicken, and some good old biscuits
that her benefactor brought. The little pickaninnies
who've gotten out of bed begin to link arms and
dance around.)

Mary Custis Lee: Old Nurse, the general would
kill me if he saw me aiding the darkies, but I want
you to know that I'm on your side and I want
you to be free. If it were left to me you'd be out
of here. And of course I'm oppressed as much as
you are. We fellow sufferers must stick together.

Our fates are intersectional. We are united in
our subalternity. Our conditions overlap.

Old Nurse: You such a good mistress—ain't she
chirren?

*(The slave children begin to sing, "Ain't she
wonderful.")*

"What crap! This woman compared Blacks to African gorillas.
She wanted to send Blacks to Africa after the war. The country
would have been better off if she and her family had been sent
back to England." Boa poured himself another drink. He was
getting tight. So was Shashi. He began waving his finger in
Shashi's face.

"What you should add is Old Nurse escorts Mary Custis to
the door and watches her as she carries her basket of goodies to
the next slave cabin. She watches her knock on the door. Old
Nurse sees a figure jumping out of the window in the back
of the cabin. A naked figure can be seen carrying its clothes
and running toward the main house. It's her brother, George
Washington Parke Custis."

"I don't get it." Shashi said.

"Mary Lee's father, George Washington Parke Custis, and
other male members of the family sired children by Black
women. Fifty percent of the slaves at Arlington, Lee's home, were
half White! George Washington's adopted son and his friends
turned Arlington into an involuntary whorehouse and to add
to this immoral enterprise, Robert E. Lee sold the children of
Custis and other White men into slavery."

"You must be mistaken. Why would these aristocratic men
bed down with slaves? Why there are statues made of marble
dedicated to the memory of these men. Aristocrats like Thomas
Jefferson and George Washington are represented at Mount
Rushmore. In my country, such a thing would never happen.

Members of the Brahmin upper classes sleeping with *Shudra* women. And I'm sure that it never happened here. Another one of your wild revisionist theories."

"Mary Custis Lee and the other White women in her circle knew about this outrage. These motherfuckers have built monuments all over the South to men who sold their own children into slavery. The women went along with it. They went along with Lee's whipping post where Black men and women were beaten into submission. Mary Lee herself sent those slaves whom she considered 'recalcitrant' to the auction block. And what kind of fucking solidarity does she have with the slaves when she sold women whom she called 'recalcitrant'? And you have her saying that the fate of the slaves and their White mistresses were intersectional. Be serious. And then you make this sick traitorous son of a bitch Lee a hero while casting John Brown as a mad man. Who is the mad man, John Brown, who tried to liberate the slaves or this fucking psycho Lee, who sent men into battles that they couldn't win just so's he could ride on his white horse and preen during parades? Contrast that with John Brown's nobility. His lawyers wanted to get him off with an insanity plea, but no, he refused and he said, 'Now if it is deemed necessary that I should forfeit my life, and mingle my blood with the blood of millions in the slave country whose rights are disregarded, I say let it be done!' Even his generals criticized Lee's recklessness and impetuousness. After the Confederate slaughter at Malvern Hill, during which nine thousand troops were killed in six hours, one of his generals said that it was not war but murder. The motherfucker was so crazy that there was such a high desertion rate that they didn't have the manpower to finish the war and toward the end of the war, Lee tried to get slaves to fight. What a psycho. How did people feel about him? Both the slaves and the White soldiers believed that the motherfucker was out of his mind. When an overseer, even a fucking overseer, refused to whip a bare-breasted Black woman who had tried to run away, because the Overseer didn't have the heart to whip this woman, Robert E. Lee seized the whip and began whipping her himself. A no-hearted motherfucker."

"My dear fellow, do you think that you have better judgment than—"

He rattled off some names of historians who wrote books lionizing Lee and defending the South and casting the war as the war of Northern aggression. The kind of historians who, if they had celebrated the Nazi counterparts of Lee, Jackson, and Johnston— Himmler, Goering, and Eichmann—would have been hanged at Nuremberg. He mentioned Shelby Foote, who compared the Klan with the French Resistance.

"You are skating on thin ice when you challenge these experts. These men have PhDs in history."

Boa, having worked in Academia, had long ago found that the PhD could be used to commit intellectual larceny. "It's expected for you to say that. You even believe that the war was not fought over slavery."

"It was fought over states' rights."

"States' rights my ass. Jefferson came up with this states' rights shit because he was afraid that Adams would federalize the slaves and without his slaves, Robert E. Lee was broke. After the war, his daughter had to beg people to give him a job."

"My poor badly educated bloke, it seems that you're just trying to impose the views of today upon those of the past. Lee, Davis, and others only reflected the times."

"Yeah, well a lot of his contemporaries agree with me, including the hundreds of thousands of slaves and thousands of Whites. In fact, in the South, there were secessions within the secession, including those who didn't own slaves and had no dog in the fight. When Lee invaded Maryland he thought that the citizens would rally to the Southern cause. In fact, the citizens of Maryland didn't cooperate and in Pennsylvania, White citizens tried to rescue those Blacks that the Confederate army was whipping back into slavery.

"Yeah, they salute Lee's sangfroid when visiting the battle-field. Sangfroid is the sign of the psychotic mass murderer. Excessive coolness in face of some of the most horrible scenes in the history of warfare. Definitely something was wrong with Lee. His father exhibited all of the signs of a mental disorder. He landed in a debtor's prison. Light-Horse Harry, a revolutionary war hero. He abandoned his family for exile. At least Light-Horse tried to find his way back to humanity. He tried to self-medicate by contemplating the Vedas. Maybe he was haunted by the pregnant slave woman whom he hanged when Governor of Virginia. Her crime? She fought back against an overseer who was assaulting her. His son, Robert E. Lee, ordered a runaway slave who had been returned to be lashed and brine poured into the wounds.

"And this shitty thing you say about slavery. Nowhere on earth were slaves treated as brutally as Southerners treated Blacks. PBS might believe that those whom they call tribal chieftains were just as bad as the British and American slave masters. Unlike Southern slavery, African slavery rarely involved hereditary enslavement. Native Americans too. Both free and enslaved Blacks would rather stay with even the racist Cherokee than be under the management of people like Robert E. Lee, even if it meant joining the Cherokee on the Trail of Tears. A result of Whites gentrifying Cherokee lands and expelling them. In those groups a slave could marry into the tribe or be adopted by a clan. In Muslim slavery, a slave could rise to become a general. The son of a concubine could become a prince. In your own country Aurangzeb, the Mughal, allowed slaves to become members of his court. During the Ottoman Empire a slave could become a sultan.

"And your argument mimicking Lee, that Black slaves would have been better off in slavery than in Africa—well how do you explain all of the slaves' ship revolts that happened because Africans wanted to stay home? Why did those, after obtaining their freedom, return to Africa?

"The difference between the Black slaves in this country and your people is that your people left Africa seventy-five thousand years ago and therefore weren't available to the kidnappers. If you had stuck around it would have been your asses stuck in the holds of a slave ship."

"Where did you get such an absurd conclusion as that? It's ridiculous."

"Indians come from Malawi. They left because of the droughts." Shashi laughed for a long time. It was a nasty laugh filled with contempt, and mocking. Noticing this, Boa plunged the words dagger into Shashi's pro-slavery argument.

"That's why your precious Lord Krishna is blacker than me. He's a soul brother." Boa said, dating himself. Shashi laughed even louder. "To add to that Krishna is Sanskrit for Black!!" He said jabbing his finger into Shashi's chest. "If he had existed in everyday life instead of in mythology, he would have been treated as an Untouchable."

Boa was stung by the contemptuous look that Shashi gave him. He staggered over to where Shashi was seated, sipping the Soma. He thought of the article Shashi wrote, suggesting a compulsory C-Scan of the brains of Blacks to determine whether the size of their brains was the source of their intellectual deficiency.

"Where do your people come up with such wretched speculation? Indians and Black people have nothing in common. We are hardworking. Your people spend all of your time eating bad food, chiseling the welfare state, and having sex with your children. It's all in that movie *Precious*. You're violent, lazy and—"

"Oh I see. You may reject Hinduism for Western modernity and Anglicanism, but you still think like a Brahmin, a so-called higher caste that has conned the other castes into believing that they're descendants of some mythical invasion. An Aryan invasion that never happened. Now I understand why so many Indians are ensconced in right-wing think tanks, and are being used against Black Americans. It's because you view Black Americans as Untouchables, you son of a bitch."

He wrestled Shashi to the floor. They began to roll around, drunkenly for a while, until exhausted, Shashi said: "Well," rising from the floor and breathing heavily, *Yeh bakbak ka unt kaisey karaoo?* Shashi thought, out of breath. "You can take up all of your complaints about the Lee musical with Boss Player," Shashi said. His kimono was torn. Boa had a small cut on his forehead where their heads had collided. Shashi had mentioned the name of a well-known Black rapper. "He's writing the music for the hip-hop opera, *Robert E. Lee, The General Who Rocked.*"

"Boss Player, the hip-hop star?" Boa said, sitting up from where he and Shashi had been wrestling.

"Besides, X and Y will be playing Robert E. Lee and Stonewall Jackson." He mentioned the names of two Black Hollywood stars. Asked by his sister-in-law if he felt any qualms about this slaughter of fleeing soldiers and perhaps civilians, Stonewall Jackson seemed surprised. "None whatever," he replied. A Civil War battle? No Mexico, where the future Confederate officers, Jackson, Lee, Beauregard, Johnston, Davis, experimented in mass murder in a cruel mismatch against Gen. Santa Anna, who deplored slavery as an evil. Why isn't the Mexican genocide ever discussed when establishment historians argue that the statues to these should remain up? When they flippantly dismiss those who oppose the honoring of men who kept their ancestors in bondage, conducted cruel experiments upon their bodies, and tortured them as engaging identity politics. Was Ishmael Reed right that Edgar Allan Poe with his torture chambers, the undead walking about after dark, and waning maidens told more about the South than the elitist historians who were Great Man Freaks? Think of the following scene as taking place in a horror movie: "he then ordered us to the barn, where in his presence, we were tied firmly to posts by a Mr. Gwin, our overseer, who was ordered by Gen. Lee to strip us to the waist and give us fifty lashes each, excepting my sister, who received but twenty; we were accordingly stripped to the skin by the overseer, who, however, had sufficient humanity to decline whipping us; accordingly Dick Williams, a county constable, was called in, who gave us the number of lashes ordered; Gen. Lee, in the meantime, stood by, and frequently enjoined Williams to 'lay it on well,' an injunction which he did not fail to heed; not satisfied with simply lacerating our naked flesh, Gen. Lee then ordered the overseer to thoroughly wash our backs with brine, which was done." Couldn't the late Christopher Lee have played Lee in that scene? "That slavery, as an institution, is a moral & political evil in any Country. It is useless to expatiate on its disadvantages. I think it however a greater evil to the white man than to the black race, & while my feelings are strongly enlisted in behalf of the latter, my sympathies are more strong for the former. The blacks are immeasurably better off here than in Africa, morally, socially & physically. The painful discipline they are undergoing, is necessary for their instruction as a race, & I hope will prepare & lead them to better things," Lee wrote to his wife December 27, 1856. Better off than in Africa. Then why were there up to one thousand slave revolts on the ships on the way here so troublesome that the colonialists in Brazil said don't send any more. And what's with this "painful discipline" shit. Was Lee a male dominatrix?

"Tell you what. I'll suggest that you be a consultant on the show. How about sixty thousand dollars?"

Boa could say no and refuse to hire himself onto a project where the producers would ignore his suggestions in favor of a box-office script that would honor Lee and bring millions of dollars to the musical's investors—he'd probably be called upon to defend the script were Black protestors to arise—or should he stick to his principles? Refuse the money. He thought about the tax penalty.

Boa supported an elbow with his hand and stroked his chin. In thought. Finally he said:

"Could you make that direct deposit?"

"I'm sure that this can be arranged. Boa?"

"Yes, Shashi."

"You never expressed this kind of anger when we were doing the debates. Why?"

"Jack said that you were the box-office draw and that I should be cool."

"Well, I'm not the box-office draw now. Hiding in the basement as a result of your generosity."

"You and other immigrants, and their American-born children and grandchildren don't know these people as we do. We can read their minds. We can finish their sentences. We've had four hundred years dealing with them. You're like those Jewish intellectuals who've made a career from denigrating Blacks. They think they're in the Promised Land now. But give it time. One of these days a Nazi clique might occupy the West Wing of the White House and from there manage a puppet clown president. Ishmael Reed predicted this would happen in his book *The Terrible Twos*. I might end up offering refuge to those who've made a career from dissing Blacks. And the Muslims. They voted for George Bush 2. What did that get them? Chaos and mass murder in the Middle East."

"You should write a handbook for second-generation intellectuals whose parents migrated from the Indian subcontinent about how to deal with White Americans. Things that they won't learn at Harvard or Yale." Shashi laughed. So did Boa.

"Maybe I will."

It was getting cold in the Oakland of November 2017. It rained a lot. The city of San Jose was flooded and there were serious mudslides in Santa Cruz. He'd provided Shashi with an Amish heater. "There are some blankets," Boa said, pointing to the closet. With that, he returned to the upstairs. He was going to ask Shashi about the treatment of women in his entourage, but was so pleased with the possibility of settling his tax penalty that he decided to bring it up later.

Chapter Seventeen

ONE NIGHT, THERE WAS some loud banging on the door. Boa was watching a special news bulletin. Si was making bellicose sounds toward "The West." When Boa answered the door, he discovered that he had been found out. Brigitte and her gang. His problem, the Canaan Syndrome, hadn't made the Diagnostic Manual yet. Oh, not the one about Blacks being condemned to "darkness, kinky hair, swollen lips," which, though insulted by Confederate novelists, have nowadays become desirable, with new aficionados attracted to them each day. The lips, the nose, and the butt. The amendment to the curse was the source of his woes. The one about an anatomical abnormality. Below the waist. In a skit about a nerdy-looking man who was dating a beautiful woman, Leslie Jones, appearing on *Saturday Night Live*, explained it as the nerd "packing a tree trunk down there." Does this mean that for millions of women size does matter? Of course the notion that Black men were macrophallic is not attributable to the Babylonian Talmud, solely. White explorers of Africa also had something to do with it.

Richard Jobson, exploring Africa in 1620, 1621, said that the penises of Mandingo men "were so large as to be burdensome to them." Johann Friedrich Herbert in 1806 remarked about their "remarkable genitory apparatus." Further evidence that Black men were aphrodisiac, with that part of them endowed with supernatural power, was the inclusion of the Black phallus in Pompeii mosaics to ward off the Evil Eye. The problem with Boa is that in his case the stereotype was true. How did he get his name? When he was delivered from his mother's womb, his member was so large that one of the nurses shouted "Boa." As in the name for a large serpent. Or the organ that Italian porn star Rocco Siffredi called "the devil between my legs." That would account for all of the breakups Boa had caused between girlfriends and even between sisters. Some were not talking to each other to this day. When he had sex with one she'd tell her sister or friend about his abnormality and they'd want to fuck him too. And when the Brigitte connoisseurs of the prominent protuberance and acolytes of the mega Ding-A-Ling found out, he was had. Women had orgasms by just looking at his "tree trunk." They wanted to feel it. To savor it. Pet it. Take it home with them. Get rid of the teddy bear and sleep besides it. When it got around that he was condemned by this burden, this brought even more problems. They wouldn't leave him alone. They'd come at night. If he hadn't escaped from the East, the Brigittes would have fucked him into bad health. No, they would have fucked him to death. Like surfers who traveled the world seeking the great wave, or mountain climbers seeking the highest mountain, billionaires gathering for a shot of brandy that costs $45,000.00, they traveled in packs to find men who were well hung. Boa had become their special target. He was considered as rare as a two-headed unicorn. He had avoided them by hanging low so to speak. An obscure professor at a community college. But now he had risked their detection by coming out of hiding. His debates with Shashi had made the national press.

Their leader, Brigitte, was standing in the doorway. One half of her was black. The other half, white. Her top hat cocked. Her legs apart. Her hands on her hips. He could see the moon over her shoulder. It was full. Her followers, the Brigittes, were flashing him some wicked smiles. They wore the same outfit as their leader with the top hat that was associated with Brigitte's brand. Brigitte pushed him into his bedroom while unbuttoning her blouse. By the time they reached his bed, she was pulling off his pants. His gland began to resemble a light bulb. The erection started moving around like a dog doing tricks at feeding time. Once both were undressed, she pushed him into a chair.

"So you thought you'd escape us, you little bitch. Nobody escapes Brigitte. Ain't that right girls." The girls laughed. He was too excited to say anything. He had learned that the best way to deal with this crisis was to lie there and let her and her associates do all of the work. She then backed into him and slid her opening down his member real slow like. She was wet. As she lowered her butt, they both made sounds that men and women have been making for thousands of years as her followers, the Brigittes, looked on in fascination as Brigitte turned him over, lifted him and pinned him against the wall fucking him all the while. Just as Yosemite reminded one that one lived on a planet, the sounds made during sex, involuntarily, reminded one that, regardless of your class, you were still an animal. After she finished with him her crew began working him over. Turning him over. Standing him up. Pushing him into myriad positions, while Brigitte having had her full of him marched around the bedroom blowing a whistle.

Shouting instructions. And then Brigitte having rested, and the Brigittes exhausted, she went at him again.

When she finished, she dressed. He was at her feet. Naked, shivering.

"Please Brigitte. You almost killed me with love in New York. Now you're out here trying to finish the job. Brigitte. Please Brigitte, baby. Mercy Brigitte. Please Brigitte, mercy. Baby. You fuck me so good. I can't help myself." Her followers laughed.

Brigitte said, "As long as you have that magnificent creature between your legs, we won't let up. In fact, let's roll him one more time, girls." They tackled him and began working on him.

Boa was saying, "No. Please. Don't. Have pity on me, Brigitte. Have mercy. Stop. Don't. Please. Don't." They left him naked and spent on the floor of the apartment. Out cold.

Chapter Eighteen

How did it begin? He was living in New York on Ludlow Street. Downtown. The street where the great dancer Sally Gross grew up. He was teaching history at an experimental college in Brooklyn. Unlike Oakland, New York was a city where entering a different block was like entering a new city. You could have one life downtown, another life midtown, and another life uptown. Ralph Ellison in his great novel, *Invisible Man*, has a character named Rinehart, a shape-shifter. In New York you could be a shape-shifter Oakland's NextDoor.com, which some called Nigger Watch, was minuscule in comparison to the New York eyes that were on you around the clock. The city that gave us Stop and Frisk. The NYPD spying on Muslims.

Brigitte was known for her "robust sexuality." That's an understatement. She was known to put a man six foot under with affection. He was extremely vulnerable. He was known to have the biggest dick below Fourteenth Street. In fact his dick was more famous than he. Had more power than he. For most men this would be a boon. For him, well it was a curse. He was a sexual Panda.

He suspected that the Brigittes' scouts noticed that trucks and cars driven by women in uniform, DHL, Federal Express, and the U.S. Postal Service stayed for an unusual length of time when delivering packages to his apartment. Some of them didn't deliver anything at all. The Brigittes, who only come out at night, had one of their daytime spies investigate. They sent a scout, dressed in a uniform, to test him. They fucked until three a.m. when she had to get back to the cemetery. They'd figured him out. What he couldn't resist. A woman in uniform. If he hadn't left New York, he would have been fucked into oblivion like Leslie Hutchinson, the love martyr. Boa traveled to California, which was dismissed by New Yorkers as a place where lotus eaters dwelled. Teaching at a small community college and living in Oakland he thought would be a perfect cover, but because he had to make money to pay his taxes, he had become exposed. And so they were back. Vowing to finish the job they'd begun in New York. He was helpless to do anything about it.

Chapter Nineteen

NEXT NIGHT BRIGITTE AND her crew returned. They were enjoying him when Shashi happened to open the bedroom door.

"I heard a lot of screaming and yelling, I thought that—" He stopped speaking when he fully grasped the scene before him. If it were a cartoon his eyes would have popped out to the floor. Nude, Boa got up from the bed and ran to the door. He took Shashi by the elbow and led him out of the room. "Please, Shashi, you don't want to become involved in this. It could be fatal."

Shashi couldn't take his eyes off of Boa's penis. Now he understood how he got his nickname. Like one had stumbled upon a bird one thought was extinct. He thought, *usaka ling shaanadaar hai!!* Too late. One of Brigitte's assistants stood before him. Shashi's eyes went from her tits down to her bountiful bush.

"He ain't one of them Indians is he?" She asked.

"No he's a . . . a . . . Pakistani friend whom I met in college."

"You sure he's not one of those Indians. They shot down that plane."

"Oh, no. The Pakistanis hate the Indians."

"I'd better return to the basement," Shashi said breathing heavily. Panting actually. Boa noticed a swelling beginning in his pants. You could tell that he wanted to get in on the action. "Shashi, you don't want any part of this. You'll suffer like me." Too late. Brigitte had snatched him and thrown him into the middle of her followers. The room was silent for a minute as Brigitte came up with a plan. Finally, she said, stroking her chin:

"We'll use you for the entree and him for dessert," she said, glancing at Shashi's erection that was trying to get out of its prison. His pants. After they stripped him, or as Shashi would say, "disrobed" him, they began crawling all over him. Shashi began to moan politely, maybe like Clifton Webb would, but then as they worked him over, started shouting *"Mujhe Bakavaas!!! Mujhe Bakavaas!!! Yah Achchha Hai!!!"* Meanwhile Brigitte pushed Boa back to the floor. Climbed on top of him and continued to gallop over his penis. She started yelling "Hi-Yo, Hi-Yo silver awwwwaaay," to the amusement of the Brigittes who were working over Shashi.

Boa always marveled at how fast they could bring a man down to his skivvies. Afterwards, he and Shashi slept for a long time. Finally they awoke. Shashi made some chai. He had taught Boa how to make it. "I never had sex like that before," he said. "What a right royal night that was! I'm used to these needle-thin blondes at the American Enterprise Institute and the Haterage Foundation. Women whose diet is cigarettes and Chardonnay. I was trying to make love to one of them who was massaging my penis, very elegantly, I might add, while reading a copy of Adam Smith's *Wealth of the Nations*. Thanks so much for cutting me in on the action, Boa. Will they be returning?"

"Yes, they'll return. They only come at night. I can't help myself. You have a choice. It's a lot of pleasure for you, but for them it's an act of attrition."

"That will be a thrilling way to go."

"It's nothing to be flip about. The graveyard is full of men who have crossed Brigitte and her followers. Like insects deprived of their insides. I am doomed but you have a chance." They drank some Soma.

"By the way," Boa said, finally. "You said that you'd never speak Hindi again. Wasn't that Hindi that you were hollering when that Brigitte blonde was giving you *Maukhik Sambhog*?" Shashi shrugged his shoulders.

"I got to get some sleep," Shashi said. Boa could tell that he was embarrassed at letting down his guard. After Shashi returned to the basement, Boa went to sleep in his favorite manner. Reading the subtitles of a foreign movie. Worked every time. Of all of the films available on Hulu, his favorites were the Korean films. They kept him awake. They had some panache.

That night, Boa had an episode of sleep paralysis, something that had afflicted him since childhood. He could not move. This time a man stood at the foot of his bed. He was dressed in what his dream mind identified as Babylonian dress. He was carrying a copy of the Babylonian Talmud. He was bearded and wore his hair long. "What did you summon me for my son?" his dream character said. He had difficulty replying because the head of the Hindi vulture demigod Jatayu was lying on his chest heavily. He was between sleep and wakefulness. He addressed the bearded man. By the way, Boa hadn't summoned anybody. But his dream self said:

"The curse that you put on Canaan. This is the twenty-first century, isn't it time to remove it? I mean nobody even knows the origin of it." The man paused. Boa could hear the dialectic bouncing around in his mind like a badminton shuttlecock. He was having an internal dialogue in his head:

It's because Ham had sex on the ark. With his mother?

No, it was because Ham had sex on the boat. With somebody else?

It was because Ham saw Noah drunk and naked and made fun of him? He caught him masturbating?

Boa tried to help him out. "Shaming."

"What is that my son?"

"*Nowadays, we call it shaming. If you look at social media, not only are people shamed, but animals. Dogs are shamed on YouTube, for example, for chewing the cover of Bill Clinton's autobiography. Ham was trying to help Noah out. Noah was an alcoholic, and Ham thought that by shaming him he'd give it up. There was no Alcoholics Anonymous in those days. Why would there be a curse on Canaan? First of all, he was innocent. As for Ham, he was only trying to get Noah off the bottle.*"

"So you want to have the Blackness part of the curse taken back?"

"*No. Being Black is really cool. Everybody wants in, that is as one Black comedian said, until somebody calls the police. You have Whites doing Black dance, Black writing, wearing P. Diddy's clothes—some of them are even saying that Whites invented hip-hop.*"

Boa could tell that the visitor wasn't following him. And even the vulture Jatayu looked up at him quizzically.

"Is it the kinky hair?" the scholar asked.

"No kinky hair is okay. Women say they get bored with the same old polite hair. They want to run their hands over hair that has character. Hair that is as wild as the coast of Northern California. That's defiant. Women from other nationalities—that's the first thing their hands go for when fucking a Black guy. Of course, you guys invented fucking women from other nationalities. Take Solomon. Besides the Pharaoh's daughter, among his foreign women were Moabites, Ammonites, Edomites, Sidonians, and Hittites. He defied the Lord's command: You must not intermarry with them, because they will surely turn your hearts after their gods.

"He didn't pay the Lord any mind when it came to good sex. He had seven hundred wives of royal birth and three hundred concubines. They fucked him so good that he left the Lord and began worshipping Ashtoreth the Goddess of the Sidonians, and Molek the God of the Ammonites. Chemosh, God of the Moabites. On a hill east of Jerusalem, Solomon built a high place for Chemosh. He did the same for all his foreign wives, who burned incense and offered sacrifices to their Gods. Gods who like the Hindu Gods were made in the images of fish and cows."

The scholar ignored him.

"The swollen lips?"

"No, women like that too. They're crazy about our pregnant lips. They say that our kissing them gives them twice the pleasure they get from men with hardly any lips at all. Men with Charlie Brown's lips."

"You men have noses that sit on your faces like a frog. You want a nose like Basil Rathbone or John Barrymore?"

"You kidding? Our wide nostrils are capable of picking up the scent of a storm a hundred miles away. It is one of the few human noses that has been political. In order to deny the conquest of Egypt by the Black Kings of Kush, the vandals and savage invaders smashed depictions of African noses. That's why the noses of the great leaders of Africa are missing in the sculpture and representations of

Black Kings. The chief God of Egypt, Osiris comes from Kush. The Native American nose is built for the same function. We will be the first to smell the apocalypse." The vulture started to laugh. Boa tried to push it from his chest. It began to make some horrible screeching sounds.

"Well my son, if those parts of the curse are not what you want me to remove, which part is it?" said the scholar, who talked like Larry David.

"The elongated part. You know—the part about the anatomical abnormality. It's caused Black men nothing but misery. Even the rumor that such a thing exists. Thousands of Black men have been lynched and castrated because of that part of the curse. In the South, they had their penises cut off and the ones who violated the corpse's body would take the penis home to cook it—some preferred broiling, others baking or frying, maybe with some hot sauce, you know Southerners, and eat it as a way of having this gift transferred to them. Must be some kind of Scotch-Irish custom. Those people liable to do anything. Benjamin Franklin called them 'white savages.' And in the U.S. women have become so fascinated with this idea that Saul Bellow and Philip Roth described the Black penis in scrupulous detail in their books in order to boost sales. Kenneth Goldsmith, in order to boost his lecture fees, did the same thing. I can't get any work done and little sleep, from Brigitte and her friends knocking on my door and following me around. They're about to worry me to death and of course I'm cursed because I'm addicted. You have to bail me out of this situation. They almost murdered me with pussy in New York. That's why I escaped to the West. Put it this way, our copulatory organ might be the most political body part in world history. It has been nothing but trouble for us. They bring us from Africa where we were minding our business and hurl us into a land where according to Kim Wallen and Samuel Candler Dobbs, Professor of Psychology and Behavioral Neuroendocrinology, about seventy-five percent of all women never reach orgasm from intercourse alone—that is without

*the extra help of sex toys, hands or tongue. And ten to fifteen percent
never climax under any circumstances. They always argue that if
they hadn't brought us here, we would have been eaten by lions in
Africa. I think that most Black guys would rather be wrestling lions
in Africa than wrestling with those statistics. In fact, I'll bet that
more Black men have been lynched because of the aura about their
genitory equipment than were killed by lions over the same period.*

    *"You have put your argument brilliantly my son. It is something
for me to ponder. I'll take it up with my colleagues."*

    Boa woke up. His pajamas were hot and wet. He couldn't get
back to sleep. He went over his last Hindi lesson. It was a poem
by Utkarsh Arora. *Undaan. Sansaar ki ranjhisho ko tod kar mai
ud chala baadlo mei kahin.* "I break from a world of regret by
flying into the clouds." Boa's flying into the clouds was through
these women. They satisfied his special desire. He'd gone cold
turkey ever since he left New York, led a Spartan and chaste life,
but now he was hooked once more.

Chapter Twenty

SINCE THAT NIGHT WHEN Shashi caught Boa with Brigitte and her followers and then joined in, Boa and Shashi had settled into a routine. The Brigittes would arrive through the back yard. They could tell that they were arriving. The dogs would howl and the cats would run away. That would begin a night of vigorous fucking.

Boa would rise at about ten thirty a.m. Study Hindi. Online. At about eleven a.m. he'd go to the basement and have breakfast with Shashi. At first, when Shashi moved in they would eat a wholesome meal. But now they could hardly lift their forks. They might even fall asleep during the meal. They might read while listening to KPFA radio. Mitch Jeserich on "Letters and Politics," which was followed in the morning by "Music of the World." Music from Africa, Asia, and South America.

One morning they were listening to the BBC, Si came on to announce that India was beginning to deliver sanctions against the United States and was encouraging China to do the same. Shashi got up and turned off the BBC. He reached for a bottle of rum mixed with red peppers. Brigitte demanded this drink. Poured a glass for himself. Poured some for Boa. "The bloke is a disgrace. He is not only making things arduous for Indians in the homeland but also for those throughout the diaspora. For decades our people have been educated in English schools, worn English clothes, celebrated Christmas, and this man Si is sending India back to the nineteenth century. Now they're talking about a database with the names of all Indians in America. There's talk of barring Indians from entering the United States, and restricting the movements of Indians who live here, even those who were born here. It's all this hothead's fault." Shashi said.

"Well from my understanding it all began with the Mountbatten scandal. He was a bālakāmuka."

"Absurd. The charges were false. The Mountbattens represented the Empire at its best. He was so resplendent even while shooting lions from the backs of elephants. Not a speck of dirt offended his beautiful white uniform. They had two dinner parties every night where the English women wore gowns and the men tuxedos. Just like the India you see on PBS. That was the golden age of India. And now. This fanatic Si."

"Yeah, well I heard that Mountbatten's old lady was fucking Nehru and there was one guy, she and her circle of royal bums and decadents like that Nazi, Edward the Duke of Windsor, and his promiscuous wife—this poor Black guy Leslie Hutchinson, a Black jazz pianist. They fucked him so, the poor guy died of a protein deficiency. He died broke."

"What on earth are you talking about? This is a dastardly accusation."

"Fifty percent of sperm is protein. Lacking protein his nails became brittle, he began losing his hair, his organs began to cannibalize each other. He and Paul Robeson fucked Edwina Mountbatten and worked their way through the royal families and socialites of England. Mountbatten didn't care. He was taking up his time fucking Indian boys. He even offered to pay for Leslie Hutchinson's burial expenses."

Shashi started toward Boa.

"Take that back."

"Take what back? It's true." Shashi swung at Boa but was so weak he missed. This gave Boa an opportunity to counterpunch. But lacking strength he fell forward. They tried to help each other to their feet but could hardly rise. They were like King

Dhritarashtra's son, who "lost his colour, a pallor . . . coming over him," had "no taste for food," and was "brooding."

"What's happening to us? I could hardly get out of bed today. I brushed my hair and a lot ended up in my brush. My nails are brittle," Shashi said.

"I warned you. We're getting fucked into obscurity."

"That's absurd. How could that be?" The bell rang. Boa went upstairs to answer. There were four of them standing there. Brigitte, their leader, an Asian woman, a sister, and a White brunette. Before this experience, Shashi said that he didn't know that brunettes could fuck.

After the women left, Shashi and Boa decided to watch a movie. Boa wanted to watch one of these sexy Korean flicks on Hulu. His favorite was *Bad Guy*, a 2001 South Korean film by director Kim Ki-duk about a man who traps a woman into prostitution after she humiliates him, publicly. Shashi wanted to watch Ingmar Bergman's *Autumn Sonata*. Boa hardly had enough strength to manage the remote. In the film Bergman was teamed up with Ingrid Bergman, the great actress, who caused a big stink in the United States when she ran away with an Italian film director, Roberto Rossellini. Another theory is that she ran away from her dentist husband because she got sick of breathing in the tons of pollution that Pittsburgh's smokestacks were lobbing into the air. It didn't work out. She even used her lines in his films to put him down. Like the film *Stromboli*. You knew when the Bergman character complains about being stuck with a stupid peasant fisherman, she's talking about her husband Rossellini and he pays her back by ending the movie with her stuck on a volcano. This guy was more interested in the Italian landscape than characters anyway. His films are travelogues. But in the Bergman film, you could tell that she wanted to upstage Liv Ullmann, one of Bergman's favorite actresses. This woman who played the daughter went through the film all weepy about her mother's sacrificing her children in order to pursue a concert career. At the end, Shashi was moved and took the side of the daughter.

"A lot of people in the world would love to have a beautiful home like the one they lived in. Millions of people in your country—they don't even have toilets. The girls have to go out into the woods to take a shit, where they get raped. You care more about the safety of one White woman than about millions of women in your own country." Shashi had stood up. Boa stood up too. They faced each other.

"That's a lie."

"These Indian women are always writing novels where the Indian men spend all of their time lusting after Caucasian women whom they see on TV. They spend hours watching TV. And I'm thinking. Why would you abandon Hindi, or Anglo Pakistani writers abandon Urdu, languages with beautiful harmonies that are so easily set to music and rhythms for English, with its guttural sounds that even the French and other Romantic vocabulary couldn't calm down? I think that I've figured it out. It's because you guys wanted to get dates with English girls."

"*Tum haiy mere tahakhāne se chaley jana jaa'o!!!*" Shashi said. Boa smiled. He had struck a nerve. After the good good fucking by one of the Brigittes led him to holler in Hindi, he was using Hindi in his speech more. "You can leave now. Get out." Shashi said. Boa started to say, *you living in my house asshole. You leave.* Then he thought about the money he would get for signing on as a co-writer for the Robert E. Lee musical. Enough to satisfy his tax debt. Of course, he had reservations at first. but when assured by Shashi that Boss Player was down as producer (which meant that he had paid to front the thing while others produced) and two famous Black actors were playing Lee and Stonewall Jackson, he figured that he was covered. He picked up his drink and went upstairs to his living quarters. He sat down at the table. He tried to get back to his online Hindi lessons. It was hard to get his head wrapped around the use of prepositions in Hindi. In fact, they were post-positions. He was getting more out of Hindu history and literature than from the Hindi language, which for him was like a UFC fighter that had brought him to the mat and held him in a guillotine hold. Puttbutt said that he quit Japanese lessons when it was required that he study Kanji, which is to English what "Jaws" was to swimmers. Boa lived in the country where most of the Black intellectual fire power was taken up with convincing millions of Whites that Blacks weren't chimps, monkeys, gorillas, and apes, which was how the ancestors of these Whites were treated in Europe where they weren't considered White. The response to these literary sermons was denial and ridicule. The back and forth had become a big marketing enterprise. Moreover, men who would never be profiled racially dominated the discussion of race and when it became the version of someone who knew the experience from the inside and someone who peered from behind the curtains, their version prevailed. But Chappie was right. No matter how difficult it was to train your brain to accept a new word order, the experience was worthwhile. He was right. You were able to view the society in which you were residing inside out. Hindi transported him to a place where people had similar experiences. All of them considered children to be rescued by White saviors like Vivaldo in James Baldwin's *Another Country.* He tries to save both the Black Boogeyman, Rufus, and his battered girlfriend, Leona. He becomes Dr. Phil, giving counsel to a married woman, Cass. Like Baldwin, an obscure poet named Henry Labouchère also saw through this strategy of the White man as a sort of surrogate father to natives and women. Sometimes poets like Kipling and Robert Frost helped to chart this responsibility, this mission. Poetry and imperialism and racism often work hand in glove. In 1899, in *McClure's Magazine*, Rudyard Kipling coined his famous "The White Man's Burden." The poem coincided with the beginning of the Philippine-American War and U.S. Senate ratification of the treaty that placed Puerto Rico, Guam, Cuba, and the Philippines under American control.

Your new-caught, sullen peoples,
Half-devil and half child
Take up the White Man's burden
In patience to abide
To veil the threat of terror
And check the show of pride

The White Man's Burden was still operative. Like the 2017 Secretary of State for the United States and the Leader of Russia meeting to decide the future of Syria without the Syrian government or a leader of the opposition invited to the discussion. A president who has been accused by critics of throwing childish tantrums warned North Korea, a member of a civilization that is thousands of years old, to "behave," the kind of advice one would give to a child. Grownups do all of the talking. Though it was 2017, we were back to 1919 when White men met to discuss the spheres of influence that they would rule over the Brown people who, being "half devil and half child," were unable to rule themselves. Rudyard Kipling's poem became famous and inspired Teddy Roosevelt, who like many White presidents believed in the inferiority of Black and Brown people. Less famous is a response written in 1899 by Labouchère.

The Brown Man's Burden

Pile on the brown man's burden
To gratify your greed;
Go, clear away the "niggers"
Who progress would impede;
Be very stern, for truly
'Tis useless to be mild
With new-caught, sullen peoples,
Half devil and half child.

Pile on the brown man's burden;
And, if ye rouse his hate,
Meet his old-fashioned reasons
With Maxims up to date.
With shells and dumdum bullets
A hundred times made plain
The brown man's loss must ever
Imply the white man's gain.

There was a knock at the door. He shut the door leading to the basement. The banging on the door continued until he managed to limp across the room to answer it. The man at the door introduced himself as Detective Smith from the Oakland Police Department. He showed his badge. And asked could he come in. Boa showed him a seat. He was a tall man. About 250 pounds. Wore a plain suit and shoes. A hat, which he removed. He wore the smell of cigarette fumes. He must have read some hardboiled detective novels and imitated the gumshoes in those stories. He was definitely noire. A Black Sidney Greenstreet.

"What is this all about detective?"

He showed him the picture of Chappie Puttbutt. "Do you know this man?" Boa paused. "Sure, it's Chappie Puttbutt. Why?"

"When is the last time you saw him?"

"We were having coffee at Peet's up on Shattuck near Fifty-first Street. You know where the Genoa Deli used to be. Why do you ask?"

"He's been missing for two weeks."

"He was in good spirits. Have you talked to Ishmael Reed?"

"We talked to him."

"He was there with us."

"That's strange. He said he'd never heard of the guy."

"What?"

"That's what he said. This Puttbutt. There is no trace of him.

It's as though he never existed." Shashi, unaware of the visit, could be heard downstairs.

"What was that?"

"It's an old house. Built in 1906. It has survived two earthquakes, but we get mice from time to time. Probably mice."

"Well, you'd better call Clark Pest Control."

"Good idea."

The detective thanked Boa for his cooperation and left.

Chapter Twenty-one

THE NEXT NIGHT, BRIGITTE and her crew had fucked them until both passed out. After they came to, Boa and Shashi rose and began passing each other a joint. They were still in their underwear. Boa was so weak that it took forever for him to roll the thing.

"Shashi?"

"Yeah?" He could hardly speak. Shashi had begun to shed that affected Forsytian accent.

"The guy grew up in Miami. He did everything right. Good family. Phi Beta Kappa. His politics were a little off the wall for my taste, nevertheless, that was shitty what you did to that Cuban congressman. Fucking rotten. Judging him on the basis of some paper that he wrote in college calling Santa Anna Mexico's Lincoln and saying that it showed his disrespect for the heroes who died at the Alamo. Heroes. Those guys were slave owners. The Mexicans told the Americans that they could have land in Tejas, but they couldn't bring slaves. Well, this outraged people like Stephen Austin, one of the trespassers. He began a guerilla war against the Mexicans with the encouragement of President James Polk, another slave trader, who wanted to annex Mexico. It's a disgrace that one of Tejas's major cities is named for Austin, this bastard." Shashi ignored Boa's rant.

"I know. The Benefactor was really won over to some crazy idea that the Hispanics were going to unite with those who live in South America and expel all of the Whites to Europe, which is in his view being overrun by Muslims and Africans. I mean you walk down the Champs-Élysées and it's like Lagos. He felt that electing a Hispanic president would begin another blow against the survival of what he called 'the favorite races.'"

"Crazy shit. The senator was one of these flag-waving rah rah boys. The kind of guy, who, if he was White, your Benefactor would bankroll. You can always find some guy who will rat out his own people. Look at Rubio. Cruz. Nunez. The Hispanic Gunga Dins. They're admired by White nationalists; they are despised by people from their own group."

"I know."

"How did you guys find out that his wife was a cokehead?"

"She wasn't."

"What?"

"The Benefactor. He set her up. Bribed some border guards to plant the drugs on her."

"What?"

"He and his club, a clique of right-wing billionaires who buy and sell politicians, were having a meeting. I was taking a dip in his pool on the roof of his penthouse and was entering a room adjoining the sauna and I heard them. They set her up."

"Why didn't you expose them? The woman hanged herself, she felt so dishonored." Shashi didn't say anything. He looked down.

"You mean—" Shashi nodded his head.

"This has to be made public."

"Are you kiddin' me? They will kill me. You don't know these guys. They were silent for a time. Some of these old guys were in on the JFK and MLK murders, Boa."

"Yeah?"

"I had nothing to do with the film. They just put my name in the credits as producer."

"Why did you let them do that?"

"The money was handsome, Boa. You can understand that."

And indeed, Boa could understand that. He couldn't sleep

without thinking of the $60,000 he owned the government and
how he was going to pay it.

"But why do you and some of the other Indians allow
themselves to be used against us. You had Indians working for
the racist anti-Semitic *Dartmouth Review*. Women who oppose
misogyny in India are given death threats, however when an
Indian feminist received the green light from PBS to do a
film about misogyny, she did one about American Black guys.
American Black guys are responsible for misogyny in India?
And then they send you guys to the *London Overseas Book
Review* to denounce multiculturalism and charge American
Blacks, who are always seen as the ring leaders of the diversity
movement, with undermining Shakespeare." *Mainey kabhi bhi
in lekhako key baare mein soonaa nahi hai(n). shaayad vah unkey
naam kaa galat ucharan kar rahaa hai(n). Naa to Hindi or naa hi
Urdu kabhi koi Shakespeare kaa utpaadan kar paayengaa,* Shashi
thought.

"Nobody is trying to undermine Shakespeare, but China,
Africa, and South America also have great storytellers. So
do indigenous people worldwide who've been telling stories
for thousands of years. Some of them are wedded to the oral
traditions (which like the Greek oral tradition, have been
translated into writing) and some write in alphabets different
from ours. Take Vyasa's *Mahabharata* and Valmiki Muni's
Ramayana, works that were written between the eighth and
eleventh centuries. Hundreds of years before Shakespeare," Boa
said.

"Two long boring video games on paper all about royals
engaged in endless warfare. Full of demons and sorcerers
and replete with long tedious monologues issued before an
opponent kills another opponent. Plots that appeal to children
without the sophisticated and complex arguments in a play by
Shakespeare or Marlowe. Next to those great writers Vyasa and
Muni's works are little more than puppet shows. Silly nonsense

about people condemned for killing cows in a former life. The bloody things are written in Sanskrit. And this reincarnation nonsense. The chief superstition of the Indian people. Just adds to the screed of superstitions that are crippling the Indian consciousness. Besides, the Bard is universal."

"The *Ramayana* has millions of followers, not only in India but throughout Southeast Asia. Why aren't these texts, which are hundreds of years old, considered classics by you? Today, Hindi is the world's third most spoken language."

"I'm not going to endorse a literature that is full of superstitious backward thought, monkey armies rescuing kidnapped women."

"Superstitions? Witches and sorcerers and soothsayers appear in Shakespeare. Hardly are his texts based upon reason and enlightenment. There are enough ghosts in Shakespeare's plays to organize their own acting company. Moreover Shakespeare, a country boy, probably subscribed to these superstitions. Racist too. Caliban barely makes it as a human. He had to emasculate Othello because he wanted to impress his Black girlfriend, a London prostitute." According to Shakespeare scholars Imtiaz Habib and Cecil Brown, his "Dark Lady" was likely an African prostitute who lived in London's theater district.

He laughed so that he fell to the floor, but was so weak that the laughter became coughs. He finally said:

"Is there any phenomenon in the universe that Black people don't regard as racist? Do you object to black holes being called that? There you go with that dreadful political correctness again. I refuse to endorse what I consider inferior literature. I would be catering to your cultural relativism. And this *Mahabharata*. In this wretched text, women can be won in crap games."

"Since when have you been concerned about women's rights? Were you concerned when you were caught with that preacher's wife in the motel? That Christian college fired you. Were you concerned about women's rights when you helped those oil barons set up that Cuban congressman's wife? That film you made about her husband? All of those lies that were carried on social media?"

"I told you that I had nothing to do with it!!" Boa's challenge rankled Shashi.

"Skip it. Look, I have to make a run. We're out of condoms, red peppers, rum. And air freshener," Boa said. They weren't buying much food anymore. Not even take out. They were beginning to look like concentration camp victims.

"I'm going with you."

"That's a very bad idea. Somebody might—"

"I'm cooped up down here."

"OK, but if somebody recognizes you, I won't know you."

"Fair enough." Shashi went into the bathroom and came out dressed in the hip-hop clothes. He'd put on some skin darkener.

"Ready?" Boa nodded. They drove to Jack London Square. So as not to be detected as an East Indian, Shashi was doing a bad imitation of a hip-hop walk like the kind he'd seen on MTV. Hunched up his shoulders and had his hands in his pockets. They walked past the Ellington condos and Everett & Jones Bar-B-Q. They paused to hear a blues group led by Ronnie Stewart. They were playing what has become known as "The Oakland Blues." Ronnie Stewart's Blues were muscular. Big Man. They were playing the hit that originated in Oakland. "The Thrill Is Gone."

They then headed west toward the FDR yacht, which the Port of Oakland had bought. Shashi read the plaque.

"The 165-foot vessel was built in 1934 and was used by the president until his death in 1945. After his death, it changed ownership from time to time and was once owned by Elvis. Drug smugglers used it in 1980. It sank and was dumped at the Oakland Estuary. It was about to be sold as scrap. The Port of Oakland then bought it and now it has become a tourist attraction."

"I'd like to take the tour," Shashi said. They went to an office where you paid for the tickets and he bought a couple. He and Boa walked onto the boat and sat down. About a half hour later, the boat began to move. It was a pleasant day and the view was panoramic. They approached San Francisco's harbor and then headed out toward Alcatraz. Shashi was reading about the history of the vessel.

"It says here that Winston Churchill and Roosevelt met on this yacht. What grand moments those must have been. It was Churchill who brought India into the twentieth century."

"What? Three million Indians died because of Churchill's policies, according to a book that I read."

"That's nonsense. Who wrote such a thing?"

"Madhusree Mukerjee."

"Never heard of her." *Kya Boa ko patta nahi hai(n) ki Bharatiya itihaas Angrez key kabzay sey shooroo hoota hai(a)? Yah ki Anzrez andhkaar mein oojaalaa lay aaye?* Shashi thought.

"Prime Minister Si says something similar. He was being interviewed on the BBC. He said that using a policy of divide and conquer, Churchill was responsible for splitting India into India, Pakistan, and Bangladesh. Si said that India was better off under the Mughals. He said that a visitor arriving there in 1665 found the country to be the finest and most fruitful country in the world. Under British occupation, Churchill used the excuse that the master race should rule its inferiors to bleed India dry, sending millions of tons of wheat and other goods to the English populations and other White nations while millions of Indians starved during famines." *Jis tarah Boa Churchill aur Mountbatten ko badnaam kartaa raheytaa hai(n), mein soon-soon kar thak gaya hoo(n). Yeh log to soormaa thay; yeh Bharat key muktidaata hain,* Shashi thought.

"That's ridiculous and this fellow Si is ruining all of the goodwill that has been built between Indians and our English mentors over the decades. I don't give a monkey about his opinion. Look at all of the damage he's done, not only in India but among the diaspora. He's someone who can't manage to keep his wig on."

"That's the result of your British education. Shashi Tharoor would call you an Anglo Indian. He says that thirty million Indians perished during the British Raj." Shashi stood up and moved to another part of the boat.

After the tour, the boat returned to the dock. They drove home in silence. Boa was so weak it took him an extra effort to place the key in the ignition. On the way home he dozed off at a traffic light.

Chapter Twenty-two

THAT NIGHT WHEN BOA placed his *bangootha* on Brigitte's *bhaganasa* he thought she was going to hit the ceiling and start to crawl around up there like in one of those paranormal movies. While Brigitte directed the action, sometimes blowing a whistle to bring the invisibles down, following her instructions, her associates began fucking them so good that Shashi fell out of bed and began to do some kind of Indian dance which he said was the dance of a Sex goddess. Tried to. Nominally an Anglican, he was opposed to the religion but felt that its arts should be preserved. One of the knocks that the British had against Indian men was that they worshipped goddesses. He made a gallant effort because he was so feeble that he could hardly lift his feet. His cardio was the pits. Before long, he collapsed to the floor, he was so lacking of energy. The three nude women kept dancing, while Boa helped Shashi back into bed. Boa began to clap his hands to the rhythm. Afterwards, the women decided to take a shower. "Now I get it," Shashi said in almost a whisper. "You can only get satisfaction from women who—"

It was then that Boa noticed a face in the basement window. He put on a robe and scooted up to the first floor. He ran to the window.

He saw a man running toward Market Street. It was Lanie. He kept falling on his ass and getting up. His big ass was having a hard time keeping up with the rest of his body. When he returned to the basement, the women were putting on their clothes.

"What was that all about?" Shashi asked.

"Nothing to worry about."

"Wasn't there someone at the window? One of the girls says that she saw the face of a man. I don't want to get you into trouble."

"You won't. Forget about it."

After Brigitte and the women left, they remained in the basement. They shared a joint as they listened to Krishna Das and his choir singing Hare Krishna. The music was beautiful. Religion has been a real problem as competing faiths had spent time attempting to exterminate one another, but the music of Christianity, the music of indigenous African religions—both on the continent and diasporic, the music and art of Islam and the other faiths show that humans are able to express their spirituality in sublime ways. God or no God. Church or no Church. Marta Vega of New York's Caribbean Cultural Center said that her temple is in her home. Orism preaches that the temple is in the mind. Ori. One feeds the mind as one would a loa, because ignorance is the greatest evil.

After going through three weeks of fucking Brigitte and her associates, Boa began to notice the signs. They were forgetting to shave. Change their clothes. They lost track of time. Experienced short-term memory loss. Had episodes of dizziness. He ceased his online Hindi lessons. He was on his knees for the first time since he had attended Chapel on the various army bases where his parents were stationed. Something that his mother insisted upon. But now he was so desperate to get rid of Brigitte and her crew that he called upon divine intervention. He knelt next to his bed. Folded his hands and looked skyward. He hadn't prayed since his teenage years. "Lord, I want to level with you the way that you leveled with your mother when she asked you about the missing butter. You need to intervene for me like you did for Sita, Lord. This Brigitte, Lord, she is a powerful entity. She got some good pussy too. Being inside of her is as if your cock is being bathed in a hot spring, a spring that starts there but then sweeps into your entire body, but the problem is that she is inexhaustible. When they said that she was robust, sexually, they didn't know the half of it. My friend, Shashi—she and her escorts fucked him so last night that I had to lift him from the floor and put him to bed. Why couldn't her search direct her to another victim? And Lord, Brigitte—she be laying those luscious hips on me and start fucking me so good that, I can't help it Lord. I ask her for mercy Lord, but she don't listen. And poor Shashi. He doesn't know what is going on Lord, but the other day he fainted Lord. He can't stand much more. Help me Lord. You have the power. A brother helping out a brother. Like you fooled that Putana, the demon of infanticide sent by the jealous King Kansa to murder you. Like you rid the forest of the donkey demon, Dhenuka. Like you killed the demon Baka who came in the form of a Crane and swallowed you, but you were so hot that he had to spit you out. But you demonstrated compassion too. You gave some of these demons whom you bested the option of redemption, Lord. This is the compassion that I want you to show to Brigitte. I'm paying for her not getting none at home from the Baron, who is not all that into women. Or can take them or leave them. Lord please help Shashi and me. And then send her back Lord. But show her some compassion. Or direct her to another individual. Some of the demons whom you bested were sent into exile. Send her back to where she came from."

He couldn't continue because he passed out right there on the bedroom floor. At about two a.m., a Nun was lifting him gently. A Nun! He didn't appeal to her Lord, but he'd take help from wherever he could get it. She helped him into his bed. He looked up at her gentle face. But then the Nun began to remove her clothes. Yes, the Nun was—you guessed it. Brigitte. In her other aspect (Google: Brigitte, then click Images). That tattoo, a red pepper she and her followers wear, was present on her thigh. Before you knew it she was crawling all over him and he was too spent to do anything about it. Little did he know that she was channeling Saint Brigid of Kildare. Brigitte was using this Saint as a cover, who in turn was a cover for a Celtic goddess, Brigid. That abbots and monks in order to woo the worshipers of the goddess merely took the attributes of the goddess and attributed them to the Saint. Like Krishna, the goddess was associated with cows. And the eternal flame. The Haitian Brigitte, who is married to Baron Samedi, both of whom preside over cemeteries, is sometimes shown as Black and White. Boadiba, one of the leading Haitian American poets and expert on Haitian mythology, says that Brigitte may be of a Swedish origin. A remnant of the fact that the Vikings reached Africa and the Africans brought Brigitte to Haiti. But there is a more compelling version. Caroline Wise writes, in her essay "Maman Brigitte, le soti nan Anglete":

> *One of the deities who appears in the vibrant synchronization of Voudoun is Maman Brigitte. Her Christian blending is with St. Bride, in whom the legend of the British goddess Brigid is subsumed. She appears in Voudoun songs, and she can ride people in rites. She is a guardian of the dead, and she manifests in the cemetery to bless the graves. It is the black rooster. She has her own Veve, a symbol that acts as a gateway for the loa being invoked. Maman Brigitte is a strong presence. She drinks rum spiced with hot peppers, which sounds rather good, and she can be jolly and fun, but is plain speaking and does not suffer fools. She has a robust sexuality and dances wildly. The spiced rum would aid all these qualities!*

So was Hirsh Sawhney right? He wrote, "Naturally, thinking is the last thing a man does when he is with a woman he desires.

Women are different. They can think anytime because nothing rears up between their legs to block the forward march of their brains." He was wrong. At least as far as Brigitte and her crew are concerned. This robust sexuality was threatening the survival of him and Shashi. He told Shashi of Brigitte's background but he dismissed it as superstition. But this was no superstition. Her Nun's clothes were on the floor.

Chapter Twenty-three

HE OVERSLEPT, BUT FINALLY awoke from his nightmare. He approached the top of the stairs. His intention was to descend the stairs to have breakfast with Shashi. He was so weak that he tumbled down the stairs. He lay there for a few minutes. No Shashi. There was a note on the table. It was written in a weak, nervous scrawl.

> Dear Boa,
>   I left at four a.m. I was so weak that I could hardly answer the door, where my friend stood, preparing to take me to Mexico. I didn't want to disturb you. He had to help me to his car. I've had enough sex to last me, well maybe a couple of weeks. I made out better than you. They'd screwed you into a state of hallucination. What was that about Brigitte living in a cemetery and the whole Top Hat number?
>   I regret that our ride on Roosevelt's yacht ended with a disagreement. For you Winston Churchill was a Hitler. For me, he rescued my country from barbarity and brought India from being a backward country to one that is gaining on China as the number one power in the world. How else would I have gotten such a wonderful education at Oxford, where I was introduced to the thinking of the brightest and the best? The greatest wisdom of mankind. I'm no chicken. Ishmael Reed, who is he anyway? I borrowed the book that you recommended. Madhusree Mukerjee's

Churchill's Secret War. Though it reads well, I cannot accept the conclusions. This book does not show the Churchill that my family has grown to love Well maybe except the family's impulsive Kala.

There would have been no progress made in India had not England intervened as one would for a sick child. But you have taught me much Boa. Information about the peculiar institution that had escaped me. The driver that was sent by Columbia Speakers says that there will be no problems in my getting past customs. My producer says that he will wire me some money until my bank account is unfrozen. Thanks again. I look forward to your working as consultant on the script, when the anti-Indian hysteria calms down and given what you have told me and what I have read in one of the books that I borrowed from you, namely, *Reading the Man: A Portrait of Robert E. Lee Through His Private Letters* by Elizabeth Brown Pryor, about Robert E. Lee, surely extensive revisions are in order.
—Shashi.

Even though they'd had fierce debates he'd grown fond of Shashi. Even missed that annoying pungent sweet-smelling scent that covered him after he showered. He missed their arguments. Yet was the real source of his services for his guest opportunism? Shashi's promise that were they to debate again, he'd receive the same accommodations as Shashi and the sixty thousand that he promised if Boa took the flak from Black protestors who would protest the musical *Robert E. Lee.* But at the same time, many Blacks would enjoy *Robert E. Lee,* if only to brag to their friends that they bought tickets that cost over $1000. And the producers were real smart to cast Black actors as Robert E. Lee and Stonewall Jackson as it was done with *Hamilton.*

He was swept with a feeling of altruism when Shashi seemed to enjoy the Biryani that Boa fetched for him. And how he neatly folded his clothes after he returned them from the Laundromat.

There was loud banging on the door. He was so tired that he had slept in his clothes. He went to the door. Oh, shit. It was the Oakland Police detective. Lanie was with him. And accompanying him were two White women from that Internet site, Nextdoor.com. It was the same detective who interviewed him about the missing Chappie Puttbutt. He had read in the newspapers that detectives had gone back to question Ishmael Reed about Chappie Puttbutt's disappearance. Reed was insisting that no such character ever existed, and indeed his name had disappeared from the Social Security Records, DMV, etc.

"Lanie says that he saw you with an Indian alien. Where is he?" "An Indian," said one of the NextDoor bloggers. She was surprised. The other one, whose pit bull had to be restrained from leaping at Boa, said, "We thought that he was one of these hoodie drug dealers."

"I saw him," Lanie said. "He was in the basement with this man and there were women. All of them were doing strange things with their bodies."

He would have been a great slave catcher in the old days. Slave catching his own people. "Plus we got this." The officer took him aside, out of the women's range of hearing. "These people are really pests but they call 911 and so we have to check it out." The detective showed him the complaint from NextDoor.com:

> *One of the remaining African-Americans in the neighborhood has been hiding another African-American for weeks. Last night a fat African-American was seen spying on them possibly from a rival drug gang. We need our members to swamp the 911 line all day in order to remove this menace from our neighborhood.*

"We need to search the place and if we find a clue that a fugitive Indian was here, we're taking you in buster." The Indian front-man for NextDoor had received an exemption for performing a vital service to the nation. There was a rumor that he was scheduled to join the other Indians who'd received exemptions in the president's cabinet. Maybe a post in Homeland Security.

Lanie started smiling with his old fat self. He was wearing his usual lavender shirt. Boa wondered how many lavender shirts he possessed. There was a commotion outside. Three unmarked cars with U.S. government insignias printed on the sides had pulled up. Neighbors had come out into the street to see what was going on. Even the White gentrifiers whom one would only see in the early morning or creeping about at night.

A plain-clothes official came through the open door. He was wearing dark glasses as in the movies. The two White women pulled on the pit bull as he lunged toward the man. He pulled out a pistol and aimed it at the dog's head. The two left the porch. Taking the dog with them. In a hurry. He said to the policemen, "We'll take it from here."

"Who the fuck are you?" The detective asked all rudely and disrespectfully even though technically he was supposed to be a public servant. He turned to the man who was wearing dark glasses and talked in a monotone like Jack Webb. When the man showed the captain his badge, the detective, who was all high and mighty seconds before, backed off and he and his men started to leave. But before he did, Boa approached him.

"Any word about Chappie Puttbutt?"

"Who?"

"Chappie Puttbutt. You came here and asked whether I had seen him."

"Never heard of him. You got the wrong guy, Buster." With that he left.

The new arrivals asked him to come with them. As they were moving out of the neighborhood toward Market Street he could see the Übers who'd invaded the neighborhood, peeking from behind curtains. He noticed the familiar cranes and workmen that had become a regular sight in Berkeley and Oakland as the cities were undergoing a digitalized makeover. Both cities were becoming organic. He noticed a sign in front of the Arab store where Lanie worked. It was going to be torn down. So were the block's other buildings. The sign read: "Coming! The Fifth Avenue Mall. Condos, Restaurants, a Gym, Yoga, Pilates, etc." They got on the freeway heading toward San Francisco. Their destination turned out to be a famous five-star hotel. The lobby was full of military people, some of whom were brandishing shotguns. The elevator took them to one of the top floors. They exited the elevator to find more armed soldiers. They approached a door, which read "Presidential Suite." The door opened and a White man in uniform was being pushed out. From inside the suite he could hear a voice. "Now don't come back here until you do what I told you to do." He recognized the voice. It was his mother.

Chapter Twenty-four

"COME IN SON. HAVE a seat." His mother clapped her hands and the men and women who were in the suite exited. Saluting and carrying on. She continued a conversation that she was having on FaceTime. She hung up. "General Puttbutt has turned up missing. Hope that she hasn't been kidnapped by those terrorists again. Like the whole family has vanished from the planet. Her son is missing too. You ever run into him out there? I understand that he lives out in your neck of the woods."

"I see him once in a while." He wasn't thinking. He was just about out on his feet. "Jesus, Mom, why didn't you let me get dressed before they dragged me over here? I slept in my clothes, I was so tired."

"I'm sorry son, but we have no time to waste in this War on Terror. And don't you be taking the Lord's name in vain."

There was a knock on the door. A man in uniform wheeled in a breakfast tray. On top of the linen cloth were two pieces of whole-wheat toast, a boiled egg, and a big coffee pot. The man poured her a cup of coffee.

"Now nuke it." The man, a huge burly White man, removed a pint of bourbon whiskey and poured a shot into the cup of coffee. Her phone rang. She picked it up. "No word?" There was a pause. "Keep me informed."

She turned to Boa. "General Puttbutt is missing. Gone without a trace. As though she never existed." Then turning to the man who had brought the breakfast tray, she ordered, "Next time I tell you to do something, I expect it to be done."

"Yes Sir—I mean Ma'am." He saluted and exited.

"We have a long way to go before these people get it right. They used to us serving them, not them serving us." There was a silence. He was so tired that he felt like going to sleep right there on the couch.

"You must be tired, the stress that came from shielding that Indian terrorist." He woke up then. She read him.

"How did I know? That's for me to know and for you to find out."

"It was Shashi, my debating partner. How could I turn him down?"

"You're my son, Boa, but you can be foolish at times. Your Dad was always worried about you. These Indians don't care nothing about you. They learned how to be racists quicker than other immigrants who came over here and were allowed to leap ahead of Black people. They learned how to say nigger in record time. That fool Si over there who is giving us such a problem right now was educated at Harvard. Half the members of Saddam's government were educated in the United States. And bin Laden's mentor? Abdullah Azzam Shaykh. This old fool came to an American campus and saw these White whores walking around half naked. He nearly lost his mind. Next thing you know, we got 9/11. You can blame these White sluts for those people getting killed. You can't depend upon these whores, the White man who is a mama's boy, and the Black man to uphold the nation. The only thing that keeps the brothers going is hating Whitey. It's their gift that keeps on giving. You see them writing these weepy memoirs, full of self-pity and making money on telling White people how hard it is to be a Black man. Look here White folks. Look at my wounds. Step right up. You can feel them for a dollar. They should go to Walter Reed Hospital. See people who really have it hard. Half their brains missing. No arms and no legs. Blind. While the brothers knocking up every woman who would lie with them, and buying steaks and champagne with food stamps."

"Mom, you tend to generalize."

"Generalize my foot. The only thing that is holding off the destruction of this country is the Black woman. We are the tit that nurtured the millions. We raised the Black man and we raised the White man while their mothers were out giving everybody pussy and having abortions because they scared to insist that their partners use a condom and when they're not doing that they training their old sluttish daughters to give away pussy. Why would anybody be surprised that the majority of White women would vote for a man who promised to grab their pussies? That didn't repel them. That thrilled them. And this new first lady we got here. How do you think that she got by when she came over here from Belarus, whatever." She whispered into his ear.

"Mom!!"

"What are you so upset about? You ain't all that innocent." She gave him a wry smile and winked. She lit a cigar. She gave him a knowing look. Could it be that his mother, his own mother, would be spying on him? He noticed Condi Rice's photo on the piano. She followed his eyes.

"She was up here this morning. Played 'Amazing Grace' for us. I love that woman."

"Yeah, what happened to the mushroom cloud?"

"Oh, I see you want a world where trash-bag-wearing thugs like that ISIS is throwing acid into the faces of girls who want to go to school or using the Yazidi women as sex slaves. Where people are exterminated if they can't recite the Koran. We Black women in the armed forces are the only ones standing tall before these murderers who want to behead America. As for these White nationalists—let them bring it. We'll send their asses scurrying back to Hillbilly heaven." She disappeared into the bedroom and returned with a gun that was as big as she. "You can bring down an elephant with this sucker." She noticed that while she was pacing up and down the room Boa had fallen asleep. She woke him up.

"Boy, what you doin' sleeping in the middle of the day? You sick? When was the last time that you had a check-up?" An aide came in with a phone.

"The president is on the phone."

"Come here boy, give me some sugar." She grabbed Boa's shoulders and pecked him on the cheek.

"You stay out of trouble, boy. No matter where I'll be I will keep an eye on you." She waved Boa away. His signal to leave. Just as he left the room, he heard her say: "The weather is fine here, Mr. President. What's the latest on General Puttbutt?"

Chapter Twenty-five

JUST AS HIS MOTHER predicted, things did change in India. Events had escalated between India and England so that Si was threatening to place a no-fly zone over London. A week later, Si was having lunch in some exclusive Delhi club before catching a plane to Pakistan to begin unification talks. He had made an appeal to the Muslims. In a speech before Parliament he talked about how Churchill was behind the division between India and Pakistan. The partition was his idea. Hindu speakers still use Urdu words.

"Tomorrow, I will meet with leaders of Pakistan to begin negotiations for unifying our people, who were divided by British Colonial rule. Whether we be Bangladeshi, Baharat, or Pakistani we are one people. We have worshipped at the same shrines and helped each other build shrines. We have worshipped each other's saints. Muslims have worshipped our Lord Krishna. Some of us Hindus have Muslim names. We have played each other's songs. Fallen in love with each other. Our ties are ancient. The Mughals, Muslims, translated literary texts including *Mahabharata*. The Colonial Jackals divided us and as Abraham Lincoln said, 'a House Divided cannot stand.' Let us look forward to a house with solid ancient grounding."

As Si traveled to Pakistan for talks, a bomb went off in mid-air. His successor promised friendlier ties with the United States. He just about took a religious vow to modernity and even hinted that he wanted to bring India into NATO. The sanctions were lifted. There was no more reference to internment camps from the president. There was an official apology to Indian citizens.

The president said that they were loyal and productive citizens who weren't on the dole and seeking handouts and rioting and committing carnage when they couldn't get their way. Indian restaurants were re-opened and were doing a healthy business. Tech stocks made a big jump as Indians returned to Silicon Valley. The black box was recovered. The plane had come down not because of a missile hit ordered by Si but because of pilot error. Some of the Seymour Hersh / Matt Taibbi types, and the kind of stuff that you hear on a KPFA show called "Guns and Butter" were suggesting that the Navy Seals had recovered the black box weeks earlier, but their conspiracy theory was that the U.S. and their allies withheld the information in order to raise worldwide resentment against Si. Of course, the mainstream media dismissed them as conspiracy theorists. Neither China, Russia nor the United States had anything to do with Si's assassination. But a nation beyond nations controlled by international oligarchs from their "nation" located on an Atlantic island bought by billionaires. Thielandia. They had contempt for rival nations. They had their own mercenary army and ruling council made up of billionaires and a few trillionaires. They avoided paying taxes in the countries where they did business and had stuffed trillions in offshore accounts. Since their hirelings, members of parliaments and congresses, had reduced regulations they were able to assault the public with bad food, bad products and bad air. Reconciliation between India and Pakistan would not serve their plans. They'd rather that they related to each other with H-bombs than with peace talks. They were guided by an obscure book called *The Camp of the Saints* by Jean Raspail, which had caused panic among White nationalists. It warned of a conquest of Europe by immigrants from India, led by a Hindu demagogue named Dung Man. An all-out nuclear war between India and Pakistan would mean fewer immigrants streaming into Europe from all of the villages up and down the Ganges.

Chapter Twenty-six

HE WAS TIRED OF Brigitte and her crew. Using him for recreation and entertainment. Pestering him because of that part of his anatomy that stood out. He decided to avail himself of the psychological services that were available to him under Woodrow Wilson's medical plan. He was so weak that when the cab arrived he had to will himself from the house. He was now using a cane. He was suffering from insomnia. Brigitte and her associates had laid such love on him that his skin had broken out. Billy Eckstine said that he was a prisoner of love, while Boa was a sex slave; his phallus was the Brigittes' target, the rest of his body, collateral damage. He was led into the office of a psychologist located in a building on "Pill Hill" in Oakland. Down the slope, toward Broadway, the Übers had established a cat cafeteria. He was led into a room. Shortly, the psychologist entered the room. She was a medium-sized middle-aged woman. She was dressed in a white uniform. White shoes, white stockings, white blouse. "What brings you in today, Mr. Bowman?"

"I thought that I'd get a male psychologist."

"You got me." She was vexed. "Why are you here?"

"Very well. My problem is sexual in nature. I'd rather talk to a man."

"If it's a problem of performance, I can give you a prescription for Viagra."

"It's not that."

"What is it then?" He hesitated. Looked to his shoes.

"My penis size."

"I don't follow."

"Brigitte and her followers are attracted to my penis, because it is oversized. To compound the problem, I've developed a fetish for women in uniform. I turn them on and they turn me on. It started out when I was barely out of my teens. The mail lady. Her crisp blue blouse and short blue skirt, big old thighs and titties aroused me. She would come by during her lunch hour and we'd make out, while my parents were off at some parade ground or something. When I was teaching in college, and lived in New York, Brigitte and her friends found out about my weakness. She and her friends are trying to bury me. Bury me with love."

"Slow down. Take your time." She was scribbling furiously.

"When the mail lady found out that I was well equipped in an extraordinary manner between my legs, she passed the word. Meter maids, policewomen, my mother's aides. There was one requirement. That they were in uniform." There was silence for a few minutes while she was taking notes. She finally gave him a summary.

"The uniform is only a symbol. Your erotic urges are misdirected. The object of your lust is Abstract. It's authority, for which women are for you, symbols. Your insistence that women be uniformed is because you don't want to assign any kind of agency to gender. You need to feel that all women are uniform, interchangeable."

"I don't follow," he said.

She began accosting him with technical language. She finally said, "And this Brigitte. Describe her."

"She and her friends wear Top Hats and they are dressed uniformly in black frock coats, when they are wearing clothes. One side of their faces is black, the other side white. They live in cemeteries."

She scribbled something down. "And when did you begin to experience these hallucinations?"

"They're not hallucinations. They twist my body into pretzel shapes and do things to me that are terrible. But—but—feel good. So good. So good. So good. And then, my friend Shashi. They fucked him so much that he escaped to Mexico, and—"

"You grew up around symbols of authority and all of its accoutrements. Medals, military bands, inspections, and so forth. And this business about women being attracted to a huge penis is a myth perpetrated by the patriarchy. A stereotype invented by racists. That you would succumb to such a fantasy exhibits some Onanism, which is also a manifestation of authority. One man rule. One man love. Why would women seek you out even if you did have a huge penis? And this Brigitte that you mention. Obviously a sign of a mental disorder. I'm going to send you over to Neuro. Have them give your brain a CAT scan. This idea that you have a big penis and are being pursued by phantoms is obviously madness. *Madness*, Boa thought. *Why would someone who was using such textbook language earlier slip and use a romantic term. Something was wrong.*

"Let me take a look at it. Take off your clothes," she said. Once he was nude, she led him to a gurney. Instructed him to lie down on it. She saw his problem. It took her a fraction of a second to slip out of her uniform. She pulled her top off. No brassiere. And then her skirt. Her white uniform was lying on the floor next to the table. He tried to rise, but didn't have the energy.

"What are you doing? Why are you taking off your clothes? I thought that this was supposed to be talk therapy," he whispered. But as she climbed atop he noticed the tattoo on her thigh. The engraving of a red pepper. A day-time Brigitte? What? He tried to resist. "No, please, don't."

But it was too late. As she pushed in and out in rhythm she started popping her fingers and singing. She was singing lyrics that sounded something like "Singing Hi-Yo, Hi-Yo Silver." The only response that he could make was a feeble sound that sounded something like ooooooooo!! ooooooooooWE!

oooooooooooooWe!! Which sounds like the OO as in Food. He was like the victim in the Delhi Noir film. Killed by sex.

> *Mukesh is introduced to "Sarika" aunty, one of the neighbors, during a get-together. He once happens to go to Sarika's home to get apples, after which he is seduced by Sarika, who uses his youthful body. She tempts him and also pays him for his services. Mukesh, when questioned by his aunt about his new-found money, replies that he earned it by giving tutions. Sarika introduces Mukesh to many such "hungry" aunts who finally make him a male prostitute.*

Chapter Twenty-seven

HE AWOKE. A DOCTOR was standing before his bed.

"Where am I?" The doctor looked familiar. He had seen him somewhere before. He wore a long beard.

"The psychologist who was scheduled to talk to you found you on the floor unconscious. You've been in a coma for two days."

"What. What are you talking about? It was Brigitte. She and her friends live in a cemetery. She is the patron saint of sex workers. She and her associates are trying to murder me with sex, don't you see. She's married to a Baron, who gives her a lot of leeway—sexually that is—and her associates, they wear top hats and and part of their faces are black and part white and, and—you must help me before it's too late." He was delirious.

"Nurse," the doctor called the nurse. A nurse injected him with a needle

A while later, the doctor said that it was okay to release him. He was dressed and was about to be discharged from the hospital. A week had gone by. His appetite was returning He felt strong enough to leave the hospital. The doctor came to his bedside.

"We took your blood and found your PSA to be sky-high. We recommend that you have surgery immediately."

"Surgery for what?"

"You have prostate cancer." Black men in Northern California have the highest rate of prostate cancer in the world. Some experts blame it on the toxic fumes from the Chevron plant in Richmond. But of course, given the fact that both his father and his grandfather had prostate cancer, maybe it was genetic.

"Prostate cancer?" No wonder he was having a problem urinating. Sometimes a trickle. At other times, he'd try and there would be no stream at all.

"What are the prospects for my survival, Doctor?"

"Very good."

"And what will be the side effects? Would I have to take pills for the rest of my life?"

"There is only one serious side effect."

"And what is that, Doctor?"

"There's a fifty-percent chance that you will be impotent. You may never again achieve an erection." Boa broke out into laughter. He wouldn't stop. He became, well—hysterical. Laughing uncontrollably. The doctor called for a nurse to bring some water. She came in. Nice butt. Big old beautiful thighs. She smiled as she gave him the water. Ordinarily, he would get a rise, but nothing happened down there. It was at that moment that he recognized the doctor. He was the Babylonian priest who visited him in his dream.

"Are you okay? For most men, this is devastating news." Boa was silent. "You can go home and return in a couple of weeks, or we can do the operation tomorrow."

"No, I don't want to return home. Please operate tomorrow. Thank you Doctor." He examined the doctor's face. "Haven't I seen you somewhere before?" Boa asked, finally.

"I don't think so." With that the doctor left the room.

Chapter Twenty-eight

THE NEXT MORNING HE was wheeled into the operation room. They gave him a drug that knocked him out. *Tritone showed up. Sometimes called "The Devil's Interval." Though he will always be a detour, like Bud Powell going from a C minor to a C# diminished in "Stella By Starlight" instead of from a minor to a dominant, the way that it's written, Tritone is the kind of guy who'd be puzzled by the fact that such a beautiful work is named for a woman named Stella. Stella could be soft, Barry Harris, or Stella could be stormy, McCoy Tyner. He prefers Jazz of the '40s and '50s to that of the present day. He broke with Jazz when they introduced Soft Jazz. He carried the bass when Diz and company performed in Paris. He was on the plane when Illinois Jacquet and his sidemen were flying home. He was in the recording studio when Coleman Hawkins recorded "Body and Soul." He was a regular at the Royal Roost. He was friend of the best man for the groom at Dinah Washington's*

wedding. He was an engineer in one of Sonny Rollin's recordings. He will offer advice for those who make awkward square moves. So he is dressed in a gray leather ankle-length coat, a leather beret, and narrow gray shoes. He speaks in riddles like Thelonious Monk. Laughs like Diz. He has been dispatched to the palace where Boa and Dion have been partying all night.

Boa was lying next to Dion. There were nude bodies of men and women strewn about the room. Satyrs were lying on their sides. Bottles of Soma juice littered the floor. "Where the fuck am I?" Dion said. Soma juice had spilled on his clothing.

"You drank a lot of Soma juice and passed out. Don't you remember?"

"Soma juice. That stuff is spiked with speed. Makes people want to fight!"

"What? Shashi and I have been drinking it like water."

"Who is Shashi?" Dion asked. Boa told him about his encounters with Brigitte and her crew. And how they wouldn't leave them alone. Dion and Boa rose. They walked out of the palace gingerly stepping over unclothed bodies. They were outside. They'd drunk so much that the brilliant Grecian sun gave them a headache. Tritone greeted them. "Boy are you two a couple of skanks. You stink. You need to clean yourselves up. You Dion, why women travel with you is a mystery to me. You wear that same old nasty goatskin day in and day out. You haven't washed your hair in years and bugs have made a home up there."

"Who the fuck are you?" Dion asked.

"My name is Tritone, master of the unexpected. At your service, gentlemen."

"Where did you come from?"

"It doesn't matter. I'm here to help."

"I don't need help," Dion said.

"Oh, I see. You're like that sucker Narcissus. Men and women were after him. Pretty boy. This Nymph Echo was madly in love with him. He rejected her. But Nemesis got even with him. He fell in love with himself. Saw himself in a pool. But didn't know himself and couldn't have himself. He committed suicide. I hope that someone stuck on himself, like you, won't meet the same fate."

Dion said, "I failed the classics and so this story is hard to follow." He winked at Boa.

"Don't play me, pal. I know your problem. Both of you. Boa, if you didn't have an enormous cock, you'd just be another lecturer. If it wasn't for your comments about Monroe Trotter, another loser, you'd still be teaching at that community college. You let this Brigitte and her friends use you as their toy. You ain't nothing but a square-assed human dildo. And this thing about uniforms. Bizarre. And you Dion. Yours is a typical Greek Tragedy. Sick plots if you ask me. Your father kills your mother and then you retrieve her from hell, change her name so that the dead aren't jealous.

What's this thing about Greeks going to fetch relatives from hell? Wouldn't you want to leave some of them down there? But I know what your problem is. First of all you're passing."

"That's a new one," Dion said. "You're the last god to make the pantheon and the only one whose mother is mortal. You have to be Black."

"You sound like Ishmael Reed and George Schuyler. Everybody is Black to them," Boa said.

"So what is my problem?" Dion asked, ignoring this.

"You're seeking revenge against your old man by trying to get more pussy than he. Forget it. He takes many different forms and catches the women off guard, like that Leda. You don't have that talent. And you Boa, you were born with a freak between your legs, a tree trunk, otherwise you would be as interesting as Hugh Downs. Not one of you can match the greatest lover who walked the earth, the baddest ladies' man who ever lived."

"*Who could that be?*" *Boa asked.*

"*He has to be pretty bad to compete with me,*" *Dion said.*

"*You see all the women in the palace there. Soundly asleep and satisfied because me and my new friend Boa here fucked them so good. Nobody can top me. These Meands, my hos, will follow me to the ends of the earth.*"

"*Aw get out. You'll never be the lover that Krishna is. The Hindu god is a lover who lures the cow girls to the forest with the sound of his flute. He is so bad that husbands have to lock away their wives, sisters, and daughters lest they will run out to the forest to make love to Krishna. The guy is modest too. These women are in the forest lined up to fuck him, the finest chicks in India, and what does he say to these women?*

"*He says, 'Ladies. Ladies. What are you doing out here? It's two a.m. and your husbands, fathers, and sons are wondering where you are. Shouldn't you be home? Suppose your infants awake and need the bottle? Or the older ones awaken from monsters in their dreams and need you to assure them that there is no bogeyman hiding under the bed? You must be out here to savor the vegetation. Enjoy the night air. Commune with nature. It couldn't have anything to do with me.' He knows why they're lined up. Yet he plays with them. Teases them. That makes them hot. They start squirming and panting. A spokesperson for the women gets down on her knees and says, 'But Lord of all Lords we love you so much. We can't help ourselves. You ask us about our husbands. You are our husband. You are the husband to all of us with your fine self and your goldan ling which finds a home in our bodies, filling us from head to feet with ecstasy. When we make love to you it's making love to a god. How can we return to these men who do the old bam bam and thank you ma'am routine and then roll over and start to snore. Please Please Please Please. Take us in your arms and fuck us all night.'*

"*And then he takes out his flute and runs through some changes and then they start to fight each other about who is going to fuck him first. One of the young ones runs to the front of the line. Strips down to her blossoming proportions and begs Krishna. Begs the motherfucker. 'Please Krishna, fuck me first.' And then he leads them to the banks of the Yamuna and fucks them all night long. With his goldan ling.*

"Well the husbands, sons, and fathers got upset. They were used to their women being anchored to the kitchen. Now the husbands had to change diapers. They had to get up and give milk to the babies. Fix breakfast for the kids before they left for school. The women would stay out all times of the night and come home in the morning. Bloodshot eyes. Placing ice packs on their heads. Breaths reeking of Nectar whiskey and Soma juice. They'd sleep all day. Once in a while their husbands would hear them moaning and squirming in their sleep, reliving the night before when they were in the arms of Krishna, and when the husbands and boyfriends wanted to make love to the women, they'd complain about having a headache or being on their period or pretend that they were asleep. The husbands, fathers, and sons had a meeting. What were they going to do about this Krishna, who had made the entire village into his own love nest? A home-wrecker. One of them suggested that they hire the demon Kaliya to deal with the intruder. They agreed and traveled to the multi-headed serpent's home on the banks of the Kalinda River. There they found the many-hooded animal busily swallowing a water buffalo. Supper!

"The serpent saw the delegation standing there. After the many heads absorbed the water buffalo they asked, 'What can we do for you?' they said in unison, swaying above them like a bridge during an earthquake. The delegation told them about how the women, their sisters, mothers, and daughters were spending all time of the night with Krishna.

"'So what do you want us to do?'

"'Get rid of him.' their spokesperson said. The many heads had a conference.

"'Fifty cows. Twenty-five now. Twenty-five when the job is done.' Deal. Well Kaliya slithered up to where Krishna was playing *his flute. The husbands, sons, and fathers were hiding in the bushes.*

"The Kaliya tried to attack Krishna but Krishna leapt to their heads and once there tap-danced on each head like he was the Nicholas Brothers dancing from surface to surface in the nightclub scene from 'Stormy Weather.' Krishna even did a couple of splits on one of their heads. The heads started quarreling among themselves other. They said to the leader, 'We thought that you said he'd be a pushover and now he's tap-dancing all over our heads. It hurts.' Quarreling among themselves, they slithered from the scene flying above the trees. They kept the fifty cows even though they didn't meet the terms of the contract. Finally, Krishna called the farmers to a meeting. It was one a.m., an hour before the women were to arrive. It was dark and stars shone above. Suddenly the night became noon as Krishna emerged from the forest.

"'Fellas. I'm moving on. There are more demons to kill and wars to wage.' The men were so happy that they began dancing around arm in arm. 'But let me give you some advice. Your women wouldn't be out here if you were taking care of business at home. Try a little tenderness. Be gentle. Be kind. You know women get weary wearing that same old sari. Overwhelm them with passion. Surprise them with gifts. Take your time. When you're making love and they say "Wait. Wait." Slow down. Women want to come too. Let them have a girls' night maybe three times a week during which you stay home and they get to go out and party. Now to show that there are no hard feelings, the fifty cows that you paid to have me killed will be returned to you. I paid a visit to Kaliya and gave them twenty-four hours to vacate the forest. If you go to their old grounds, you'll find the cows there.' With that he began to leave for another town where his services were needed. The men waved until he disappeared in the distance.

"Now Dion, compare Krishna's acts of forgiveness with your heavy-handed malicious methods," Tritone said. "You got into King Lycurgus's head, the guy had your whores, the Maenads, arrested for soliciting but your revenge was disproportionate."

"How?"

"First you sent a drought, which even your fellow gods thought over the top. Then you caused Lycurgus to murder his son mistaking him for a patch of ivy. Your condition for lifting the curse was for the people to murder the King. That's what the party last night was all about. The twelve bands. Soma juice. People were dancing. And it all ended in a grand orgy."

"Criticism well taken, Tritone. I got to get ahold of my brain. These voices. They tell me to do these things. I need help," Dion said.

"Oh, yeah. Blame it on the voices. How lame. You two know the story. Both of you should go bathe in that river over there. On the embankment there are some white clothes laid out for you. And sandals. And some Dudu-Osun. Soap of the gods. You need to go to Vrindavan Forest. Heal yourself of those voices, Dion and Boa. Boa, I promise that Brigitte will leave you alone."

"Where is it?"

"It's in Bharat."

"How do we get there?"

"This Eagle, the vessel of Vishnu, will show you the way." And indeed perched on a limb of the Kadamba tree was a large Eagle. The Eagle started toward the river. The two followed.

Boa awoke, screaming, "Vrindavana!! Vrindavana!"

A nurse stood before his bed. She was wearing a white blouse, white skirt, white shoes and stockings.

"You did well. The operation was a success." Again his penis didn't shoot up at the sight of a beautiful woman in uniform! Could it be that it would remain quiet down there? Normal. Could it be that he had finally been freed by the Dragon of Carnality, so to speak. Could it be that organ called by James Baldwin "the terrible muscle," or the "curse" between one's legs, was at peace? Would Brigitte and her friends stop showing up at his house demanding orgies?

Chapter Twenty-nine

AFTER THE SURGERY, HE spent four days in the hospital. When he returned home he opened his email. One was from Shashi. He read the email:

> Enjoying myself so much that I hate to return to the States but return I must. I'm writing this from the hotel's business center. Columbia hired a discreet stringer who drove me to Mexico. When I arrived I was dehydrated and felt weak, but since then I have spent time going from my room to the dining room. I've gained some weight. You were right about Brigitte. It was the best sex that I ever had but she and her posse were weaponized sex. I'm glad I got out of there. I thought that I would have to remain here until it was safe to return to India, but now that the crisis is over and things have returned to normal, I'll be heading back to New York. I have had a lot of time to think and during the time, read the book you suggested by Shashi Tharoor. Here again the author's wild claims about Churchill are not substantiated. I was delighted to learn that FDR was very sympathetic to the rights of Indians. But I'm beginning to understand Si's desire to unite Pakistan and India. The longing so beautifully captured in the poem by M. C. Gupta, "*arsaa ho gayaa ujde hue wo pyaar ki / magar phir bhi tasavvur mein mere basne se lagte ho.*" "Though it's been ages since our world of love was destroyed / thoughts of you still

linger in my heart." He saw Pakistan and India as lost
lovers, separated by the British.

Boa didn't hear the Gupta lines. He was still angry about FDR's
sympathy for Indians, but whose attitude toward Blacks was
benign neglect. *Just like a liberal,* Boa thought. *For them distance
makes the heart grow fonder. They're worried about the foreigners
imprisoned in Guantanamo as a result of their testing White
supremacy in these wars they're always getting into. The police
departments and prisons deliver Gitmos to Blacks 24/7.*

> Boy, have I been misled. You were right about Robert
> E. Lee, too. I've notified the Benefactor that I have
> decided to abandon the Robert E. Lee project. He
> was a truly terrible person. I met another billionaire
> in the hotel here. He is the one who is preventing a
> major newspaper from filing for bankruptcy. I have
> sold him on another idea. A hip-hop rap opera about
> the dark Lord Krishna. In this version Krishna is a Jazz
> musician. He plays flute like Jerome Richardson and
> Roger Glenn. His lover is a wealthy Black socialite. I
> know that traditionalists will have a problem with my
> re-interpretation of Krishna, but as an artist, I believe
> I should have the kind of freedom that was available
> to Shakespeare. I'm working on the book now. Got a
> call from Columbia Speakers about our slavery tour.
> I told them that I wanted out. They reminded me of
> our contractual obligation. I suggested a compromise.
> I convinced them that we should do one more debate
> and call it quits. I hope you agree. Are they going to
> be in for a surprise.

Obviously, Boa had been a bad influence on Shashi. The email
had a video attachment. He opened the attachment next.

Shashi was sitting poolside with a number of Mexican beauties surrounding him. They were dancing to Raven Symone's "I Got Mexico."

> *I'm eating right and I'm living good*
> *doing everything I said I would*
> *I should have left a long time ago*
> *who needs you, I got Mexico*

The video attachment showed a poolside party at a five-star hotel celebrating Shashi's buying uniforms for the Mexican Women's Soccer League. But these beauties weren't wearing uniforms. They weren't wearing much of anything. But the thing about the uniforms was disturbing. Had he passed his fetish on to Shashi? He remembered his first encounter. An encounter that haunted his life.

Chapter Thirty

HE WAS FOURTEEN YEARS old. Coming into manhood. He had a father who explained to him the source of his nocturnal emissions. His mom and dad being army officers had taught him how to compartmentalize things and so he placed his issues of *Playboy, Black and Tan, Jive,* and *Bronze Thrills,* etc. in a place where they would never be found. They had a house located on an army base in Texas. On the Fourth of July, his parents were away performing in some kind of patriotic ritual. He had the house to himself and was heading for his *Playboy, Bronze Thrills,* and *Jive* collection when there was a knock on the door. It was Mathura, the mail lady. People called her Matty. She was standing there. Her light blue blouse partially opened allowing a peek into those prodigious tits. Or as the poet Chandidas put it, "Her breasts rebelled against her dress." Her hips hugging the tight-fitting navy blue skirt. It was clinging to her like the skin of an apple clings to its meat.

"You have to sign for this package?" She smiled. It was when she shifted her posture that he got a little hard. She noticed and smiled again. He signed the receipt, his hand trembling. She noticed that too. He began to sweat. His erection was so prominent that he could hardly move. She smiled.

"You got some ice water?" she asked. He guided her into the kitchen, his eyes following that majestic butt as she walked ahead of him. His cock was really swollen. So hard he walked as though with a limp. He showed her a seat. After sitting, she crossed her legs and the hem of her skirt climbed above her knees. He almost dropped the pitcher of ice water that he had taken from the refrigerator. When he brought the glass to her, he said, his voice trembling, "I hope that you don't mind that the ice water is spiked with lemons . . . a . . ."

But before he could continue, she'd grabbed his dick. Zipped his pants brought it out and tried to get her hand around it, an impossible task. She was startled.

"Boy, what you got going on down there. Let me see?" He tried to answer but he was stuttering. She examined it like a taxidermist would inspect a jewel. "My goodness boy, where did you grow that thing? *E yi ye mede.*" She began to unbutton her blouse until those black beauties popped out. They seemed to say hello.

"I don't know whether I want you to stick that big thing in me." He was panting, his whole body was quivering.

"I have to get back to work so this has gotta be quick." By that time he had been reduced to mumbling. She spread herself right there on the kitchen table and pulled him into her with both hands. She was so black that she was plum purple. She brought him into her slowly. Deep into her. His dick felt as though it was wrapped up in hot wet silk. "*Di! Di ! Di!*" She was bilingual. An immigrant from someplace in the Caribbean. She told his parents once that delivering the mail come rain or shine was a sacred oath for her. She must have devoted such a work ethic to her Kegel exercises. Because she had developed her vaginal muscles. She was milking him and every time she used her muscles to squeeze his dick gently he would come.

"*Me nipadua ye wo dea.*" He didn't understand a word she was saying. He ignored her words and kept riding and plunging ahead. She really was hot and wet. "*Few m' ano! Few m' ano!!*" He hadn't the slightest idea of what she talked about until she showed him. She grabbed his head and brought her lips to his. She put her tongue into his mouth and moved it around. They were going at it and he tried to muffle her cries, but she was not to be silenced, in fact she began to shout. "Oh, God! Shit! This feels so good! *Ka Mae Tweba!*" Their naked bodies were slippery. He stuck his dick into her warmth one more time. She held him tightly until he came so hard that he started convulsing. You'd think that he had epilepsy or something. Afterwards he was calm. Peaceful. She was stroking his back and his buttocks as she held him. It was so beautiful that he almost started to cry. But these were tears of joy. How did Utkarsh Arora put it? *"Sabki khushi ko bayaan karta aankho ka vo ishaara hoon mai."* Finally, she patted him on his back.

"Get up boy, I have to go." She calmly put on her clothes. She smiled at him again. At the door, she told him, "Boy, you got a million dollars between your legs. I'm going to spread the word." She picked up her mail bag and left. He cleaned up the kitchen table. Went into his bedroom and flopped onto the bed. It was about one in the afternoon. He hadn't experienced such peace before or since this encounter. He was like the eagle in the poem, "Kasol" about a beautiful mystical place in India, of rivers and mountains, where nomads, saints, and Babaji go to seek wisdom. The eagle wanders into this land by accident but after returning home goes back. He could never go back to the situation that existed before having sex with her.

He was awakened by his father, General Puttbutt. "Wake up boy. What you doing sleep this time a day. Aren't you going with me and your mom to the fireworks display tonight?" He wanted to tell his father that he'd already had his fireworks. In his pants. As Shashi would say in his Forsytian style, he had been "positively smitten."

After that she came when his parents were away doing drills or marching up and down somewhere or receiving or bestowing medals. She took him to school and her cardinal rule was one he would never forget. "Stamina, Boa. Stamina." She had him hooked. She was the one who broke off the relationship. She said, "I love my husband. *Me da me okunu.*" He had spent years trying to capture that afternoon. While making love with her, the one who branded him with this peculiar problem, he had visions of waterfalls. It was like a scene in a Rossellini film. The kind of director who would have a couple beginning to make love and then cut to waterfalls. What is it about water and artists? Baldwin's another one. When his characters are making love he often invokes images of water. He'd never felt such peace before or afterwards. The ones who branded him with this particular sexual fetish would bring maybe a Teddy Pendergrass album. Guided by these Black crooners—Billy Eckstine, Arthur Prysock, Johnny Hartman, Johnny Mathis—you didn't need much foreplay. He tried it on the others. Maybe Big Jay McNeely belting out, "Is There Something On Your Mind?" After a few choruses from these lusty singers, the women were lubricated for the entry of the monster with which he, unfortunately, had been born. Or as Baldwin wrote: "She opened her gates and let the King of Glory in," or something to that effect. But it wasn't the same as his first sexual encounter. Unlike the transients in his life, his first love took him to the university of love and matriculated him through the corridors of passion (so to speak). He was seeking that one woman who would deliver him from the problem, a problem located between his legs. What he had learned however kind of matched up with an observation about women made by the poet Chandidas. "Who can know / The creation-woman? / Even the god/who brought her into being / has no clue at all / Poison and nectar / Were blended into one." Or as Detective McPherson, played by Dana Andrews in the movie classic *Laura* said, "Dames are always pulling a switch on you." He must have slept three days after arriving home. He got up and took a bath. In the tub, he usually got a huge morning erection. But instead, it took him a while to find his penis. He looked everywhere. Maybe it was hiding under the washcloth. No. His towering Sequoia had become a Bonsai tree. He thought of what Martin Luther King, Jr. "Free at last! Free at last! Thank God almighty we are free at last!" had preached.

There were construction noises as out-of-town developers began the construction of The Fifth Avenue Mall where the Arab store, laundromat, and beauty parlor used to reside. He ran into the Black kid who was hired by Columbia Speakers to drive Shashi and his party around. He was with one of the Indian women who was a member of Shashi's entourage. But she wasn't dressed in the costume that she'd worn when they were on tour. She was dressed up in GUESS, and wearing Ray Bans. Fashion and politics go hand in hand. The wrong colors could get one killed. The right-winger Le Pen was against Muslim women being covered at French beaches. Black women were fired because of their hairstyles.

"Hello, Professor," he said with a half grin. Boa didn't want to pause for a conversation, but was curious about what had happened to the rest of Shashi's party. He told Boa that they had been deported the day after the melee that took place at the San Francisco debate.

"What about her?"

"She's staying with me. She doesn't want to return to Shashi's entourage."

"Why?" He started to say something but the woman put a finger to her lips, a signal for him not to proceed. "You have a naive vision of India, Professor. Like W. E. B. DuBois and Langston Hughes." With that they walked on. Hand in hand. The next day, Boa went to Marcus Book Store. He asked Blanche Richardson to direct him to a book about the Untouchables of India. He selected *Dalit, The Black Untouchables of India* by V. T. Rajshekar. What he read shocked him. The Black Untouchables of India were treated by the Brahmins worse than the Blacks of America? Was this the same India that produced Gandhi, who having influenced Martin Luther King, Jr. was viewed as a saint to millions of Black Americans? Their Hinduism a model of tolerance and nonviolence? Of the Untouchables Rajshekar writes: "These Untouchable Hindus were denied the use of public wells and were condemned to drink any filthy water they could find. Their children were not admitted to schools attended by the caste Hindu children. Though they worshipped the gods of Hindus and observed the same festivals, the Hindu temples were closed to them. Barbers and washermen refused to render them service. Caste Hindus, who fondly threw sugar to ants and reared dogs and other pets and welcome persons of other religions to their houses, refused to give a drop of water to the Untouchables or to show them one iota of sympathy. These Untouchable Hindus were treated by the caste Hindus as sub-humans, less than men, worse than beasts. This picture is still true in villages and small towns."

He could not believe what he was reading. His reading was interrupted by a clunk, which meant that the mail had come. The letter had arrived from the U.S. Treasury. He owed $60,000.00. At the top, someone had written in longhand: "hehhehheh."

Chapter Thirty-one

THERE WERE INDICATIONS THAT Shashi had come through with his promise that in exchange for hiding him, Boa would receive better accommodations. Instead of taking a cab, he was transported to the Oakland airport by limo. He was booked in first class. He'd brought some reading material. He still hadn't gotten over the shock that India, a model for liberty-loving Blacks elsewhere, oppressed Blacks in their country. Forbidding them from reading and writing. In 1919, W. E. B. DuBois said: "The sympathy of Black America must of necessity go out to colored India and colored Egypt." He also said: ". . . Negroes and Indians realize that both are fighting the same battle against the assumption of superiority made so often by the white race." And when Langston Hughes said "For I am also jim crowed— As India is jim crowed by you." Was it that simple? Could it be that the British White supremacists were mere students of an Aryan Brahmanism that originated in India!! "We want to impress our foreign comrades that the founders of Fascism like Nietzsche, Max Mueller, etc., have acknowledged that they borrowed their race theory from the sacred scriptures of the Aryan Brahmins. *Adolf Hitler only implemented the Aryan race theory.* Herein lies the secret of Brahmin admiration of Hitler. Therefore Aryans, the founders of this Fascist theory of 'purity of blood,' are the real fathers of Fascism. *Hitler's swastika is borrowed from the Brahmins. The RSS symbol is also a swastika.* Fascism may be dead, but Aryan racism is still wreaking havoc throughout India, and the Black Untouchables, who are racially different from the Aryans, are the worst sufferers of this race hatred," V. T. Rajshekar wrote.

Adolf Hitler was a follower of Brahmin Aryanism that originated in India. He said: ". . . [the Aryan] is the Prometheus of mankind, from whose shining brow the divine spark of genius . . . [with which] he subjugated inferior races and turned their physical power into organized channels under his own leadership, forcing them to follow his will and purpose." Had Hitler admirer Winston Churchill received his Aryan attitude toward Indians from Adolph Hitler, who was admired by the Brahmin ruling class?

Churchill said: "I have always said that if Great Britain were defeated in war I hoped we should find a Hitler to lead us back to our rightful position among the nations." (Winston Churchill in *The London Times*, Monday, November 7, 1938) Could it be that those who were victims of British Occupation had given the British the justification for their oppression? Could this be Karma?

What was even more disturbing was that some of those who had been billed as "great minds," whose faces adorned the buildings of American libraries and other institutions, whose very names, when appearing on college and university reading lists, caused panic among undergraduates, had contributed to this hoax. In their zeal to challenge Judeo-Christian values, they engaged in intellectual balderdash. Schopenhauer, Hegel, who believed that there was some connection between Indians and Germans and even called Indians the colonizers of Europe. That "White" Aryans were somehow the progenitors of the German race, so eager were they to distance themselves from Jews that they embezzled the Aryan myth, which amounted to passing. They were attempting to disown their Barbarian past. A description cast upon them by Tacitus. And what about roly-poly cigar-smoking and porcine Churchill? He was no blond beast, either. He had black hair and short legs like Hitler. He would never have been photographed without a shirt. One of those who questioned the Aryan invasion theory was Bhimrao Ramji Ambedkar, in his 1946 book, *Who Were The Shudras?* He said of the theory that it was "so absurd that it ought to have been dead long ago." He was right.

The myth had collapsed under scientific scrutiny in the form of study released on September 25, 2009, in *The Times of India*:

> *A study was published by* American Journal of Human Genetics *in its issue dated December 9.*
>
> *The study effectively puts to rest the argument that south Indians are Dravidians and were driven to the peninsula by Aryans who invaded North India . . ."* *The study concluded that ". . . people all over India have common genetic traits and origin. All Indians have the same DNA structure. No foreign genes or DNA has entered the Indian mainstream in the last 60,000 years,"* *proving that "the Aryan invasion theory is bunkum."*

In his *A History of the Sikhs*, Khushwant Singh wrote: *"Another result of the Aryan settlement in India was the birth of the caste system. The tall, blonde, and blue-eyed invaders devised this system to maintain the purity of their race and reduce to servitude the dark-skinned inhabitants among whom they had come to live."* Was he wrong?

Ambedkar was born into the Dalit caste. He experienced the Jim Crow that Blacks experienced in the segregated South. Only worse. The Dalit children received little help from their school teachers. They were not allowed to sit inside the class. When they needed a drink of water, someone from a higher caste had to pour it. The statistics for India's Dalits are grim.

> *According to a 2010 report by the National Human Rights Commission (NHRC) on the Prevention of Atrocities*

against Scheduled Castes, a crime is committed against a Dalit every eighteen minutes. Every day, on average, three Dalit women are raped, two Dalits murdered, and two Dalit houses burnt.

This explained racism against Blacks in Silicon Valley. This explained the former Governor of Louisiana who, out of spite, refused to expand Medicaid for the poor and like Reagan turned the mentally ill out into the streets. This explained the former Governor of South Carolina, Nimrata Randhawa, a Marathi Brahmin, who was all for the Confederate flag until she was confronted with such horror over the murder of nine Christians. This explained the new Indo-American FCC chairman, of Brahmin origin, who wanted to make it more difficult for poor people and prisoners to have access to the Internet and tried to penalize a comedian who made a joke about his master, President Kleiner Führer. This explained the Indo-American students at the University of California who invited far-Right entertainers, hoping to stir up trouble, a student prank which led to violence. This explained the fucking Brahmin, the current darling of the New York Literary Establishment. who took down Richard Wright in the pages of *The London Overseas Book Review.* Like a dog retrieving a ball for the entertainment of his masters *Native Son* will be around long after this current token has been replaced by somebody else. For these Brahmins, fake and otherwise, Blacks are Dalits. Untouchables. How did Ronald E. Hall, author of *An Historical Analysis of Skin Color Discrimination in American Victimism*, put it? "Bringing their Indian cultural views with them to America, the potency of an immigrant Indian Asian's disdain for persons having dark skin only increases in their new but also racially stratified environment. Their willingness to discriminate based on skin color may then facilitate an assumed advantage if such persons interact with Westerners who hold similar views."

After a restful night at the Pierre Hotel, Boa was driven
uptown to the site of the debate. Shashi greeted him warmly as he
passed him by, en route to the suite that the Columbia Speakers
Bureau had provided for him. Startling the members of his
entourage, those who hadn't been deported, he actually hugged
Boa. "Shashi we have to talk. About the Untouchables—" But
Shashi's admirers jostled him down the hall.

Five minutes before the beginning of the debate, a theater
aide came to get them. As they walked onto the stage, Shashi
received a standing ovation, while Boa was booed. The moderator
gave Shashi a very flattering introduction while using an intro
on Boa that was dated by about twenty years. Shashi rose. He
looked toward Boa and smiled. The moderator, a tall White man,
introduced them with the predictable response from a crowd
that could afford to buy tickets. Looking toward Shashi, he said,
"I cannot add to the sentiments expressed by the president in
his address to the nation last night. Momentarily, we Americans
lost our heads when we confused the actions of a madman, Si,
the late Indian dictator, with the sterling reputation of our Indo-
Americans who are so passive that they wouldn't harm a fly.
Too busy with their heads buried in computer screens to cause
mischief. While others are unassimilable, our Indo-American
citizens blend in nicely with our Anglo mainstream. In fact,
there is no difference I shall say between them and us Whites."
With that line, the crowd rose and gave a standing ovation. "In
fact, two of them are dating my daughters," a remark that was
greeted with light polite laughter. He looked over at Shashi.
He was expressionless. "Our Indos are performing a valuable
service by keeping some of those troublesome minorities in
line. And now Ladies and Gentlemen, we will now begin our
debate." Shashi approached the podium.

"Ladies and Gentlemen, this is the last of our debate series
about the question, 'Was Slavery All That Bad?' I know that
you expect me to make my argument in defense of slavery, but,

because of those horrible days during which our community was under attack, I found out who my true friends were. 'Nobody loves you when you are down and out,' as Bessie Smith says and I found that to be so true. My debating partner Peter Bowman has opened my eyes about slavery, this peculiar institution as they called it—well indeed it was a peculiar institution—" but before he could continue, he clutched his chest as bullets ripped it open. What sounded like firecrackers preceded his seizure. He fell backwards. Boa rushed to his aid. Held his bleeding head in his hand. People were screaming and heading for the exits. They finally brought in a stretcher. Shashi was holding Boa's hand tightly. Shashi tried to say something but gurgled instead on his blood. The paramedics placed an oxygen mask on his face. They lifted the stretcher and began to leave the auditorium as the remaining members of the audience stood in stunned silence as the assassin, his shirt torn, was taken from the auditorium. His face was bleeding where the security guards had punched him. Outside, Shashi was lifted into an ambulance. Boa climbed in. One of the paramedics tried to bar him. He pushed him out of the way and kneeled next to Shashi's stretcher. His chest was a bloody mess. Suddenly Shashi pulled out an envelope and handed it to Boa. He rose up and whispered something in his ear. Boa made note of it. Then Shashi fell backward. They tried to revive him. But it was of no use. *The New York Weekly Anglo* blared the next day: "Ex Cuban American senator, Carlos Christo yells, 'You ruined my life . . .'" There was a front-page photo of the ex-senator Shashi's assassin, being wrestled to the ground.

Chapter Thirty-two

BOA CALLED KALA AND asked her to come to his home. He wanted to show her the note that the dying Shashi had handed to him. She said she'd be there within forty-five minutes. He decided to buy her some refreshments. Impress her. There was nothing in the refrigerator because he and Shashi had a habit of ordering their meals, or shopping small. He drove to Grand Avenue where some new coffee shops had popped up. He found one that just about appeared overnight called "The Grand Central." There were some Übers lined up for ice cream and lattes. When it came his time to order, the blonde woman at the counter, who had been helping other customers, stepped aside. A large Black man appeared as if out of nowhere. It was Lanie. Since the Arabs sold their store to an out-of-state developer, Lanie had gotten a job as a screener whose job was to protect stores in Berkeley and Oakland from troublesome Black men. A number of schizophrenic Black men, victims of the Reagan/Schwarzenegger legacies, were known to wander into these stores and cafes and annoy the customers. It was a new form of patrolling but the patrollers were Black and Latino. But then maybe they weren't too far off when mixing up Black men who had no access to medication and "normal" Black men. Both wore different faces for different situations.

Lanie asked him what he wanted. Boa ordered a chai latte. Though he took the order, like the Black men who had the same assignment at Starbucks in New York in the West 50s, he wasn't allowed to ring up the sale. Lanie was no longer cross with Boa.

He looked beaten. Whipped. He had the woeful eyes of those mistreated dogs in the public-service announcements. Boa felt sorry for Lanie. So pathetic.

Once back home, he heard the roar of Kala's motorcycle pull up. Her boots coming up the stairs. The ringing of the doorbell. He opened the door. She held her helmet and tossed back her black hair, which was a perfect match for the color of her face and body. He escorted her into the living room. She looked around.

"My brother lived in this dump?" She sat in a chair. Removed her glasses and swung a leg over the chair's arm.

"No, he lived downstairs." She rose from the chair and began to inspect some of the art on the wall. Huano Hakusho's *Geisha Girl*. An original sketch by a famous Spanish artist that he'd bought for $3000. The poster of Angela Davis by Rupert García.

"Would you like some chai?"

"Chai. You know about chai?" He headed into the kitchen and returned with the chai latte and laid it before her.

"I know that the place looks bare. That's only because I haven't lived here long. It needs work, I—"

"What's this?" She pointed to a work by Charles Alston. It was a mural that showed the many tasks performed by early California Blacks. They were employed as whalers, gold miners, Union soldiers, entertainers, Pony Express riders, Civil Rights leaders, convention goers, builders, workers on the Golden Gate Bridge, ministers, engineers, architects, and editors of the newspaper, *The Elevator*.

"I love the colors in this work and it's drawn beautifully. What became of the painters of this generation?"

"Some of them abandoned the mural style and became abstract painters where technique was more important than the object. One could say that they were driven into silence, when they succumbed to the demands of White-run museums."

"So why did you call me?"

"Your brother left a note." He handed the note to her. He'd removed it from a blood-stained envelope.

"It's how he wishes his funeral to end. His being controversial, he was always receiving death threats and was prepared for some crackpot taking a shot at him." She studied it for a minute. He could tell that the contents surprised her. Once in a while, she laughed.

"I can't believe this. What happened to him? Shashi was so formal. Stiff. This is a side of him that I never saw. A sense of humor. Irony."

"We spent a lot of time discussing matters while he lived here. We educated each other. I even took an online course in Hindi." She looked at Boa and burst out laughing. "Well it's a good thing that you took him in. Otherwise, he'd have been out chasing skirts. He was a notorious womanizer. Those women in his entourage? They were there to service the men in Shashi's entourage."

"What? Shashi? He just about took a vow of celibacy when he lived here." She eyed him skeptically.

"They're from the lower castes. For them traveling with Shashi was a step up. Otherwise they'd be hanging around temples, selling their bodies."

"I don't follow."

"The women do *Dhamada*. They are a human offering to the goddess Yellamma. They function as prostitutes in the service of Brahman men like those in Shashi's entourage. They are called *Devadasis*. It goes like this. A local priest pretends to be possessed by the goddess Yellamma and selects a woman to service the desires of wealthy Brahmin men. These men bribe the priest so that he will select the most beautiful of village girls to serve them. If her family refuses they tell the family that Yellamma will destroy them. And these poor villagers who are superstitious believe them. Of course, those in Shashi's entourage were lucky. They get to live a luxurious life. Five-star hotels. Fancy meals.

CONJUGATING HINDI

He and that entourage of fake Brahmins. I detested those people. The women weighed down with fake jewelry. The men Shiny and superficial. Leeches. They were always trying to get into my pants. And when I turned them down they called me a *samlaingik stree*. They exploited Shashi. He was so innocent." She began to cry softly. She composed herself and continued.

"In India, women are bartered by their fathers. The *Dharma Shastra* instructs women that they should be servants to their fathers, husbands, and sons."

"What?"

"Arranged marriages. The fathers peddle their daughters the way a pimp would peddle a whore and here was my oldest sister with a PhD mind you, with a great career ahead of her; my father sells her off to a drunk who beats her.

"India is the capital of male misogyny. Six hundred thousand unwanted girls were aborted last year. Those who are born are often drowned or buried alive. In India they care more about cows than women."

Which made it even more puzzling that when provided with an opportunity to do a documentary about the abuse of women, a filmmaker of Indian ancestry blamed Black American men for misogyny instead of addressing the cruel treatment of women in India. Similarly, Caitlin Flanagan, an Irish American feminist, wrote in a magazine owned by Oprah Winfrey that Black men were cruel to Black women. Do you suppose that she could persuade Irish American men like Bill O'Reilly and Sean Hannity to co-write a manual that would guide Black men about the proper way to treat women?

It wasn't until the 2016 election that it became obvious why 44 percent of educated White women, some of them grounded in French patriarchal theory, had singled out Black men to take the rap for misogyny, while voting for a White male patriarch who just about ran on an anti-woman platform. As Bernardine Dohrn said on Pacifica radio, they chose race over gender. Was their singling out Black men with the hatred of women while voting for a guy who was like Bluebeard to women an act of racism? The older one gets the more one realizes the complexity of human behavior. Even though a number of disciplines— Anthropology, Sociology, etc.—had investigated the species, they will discover what lies beneath Enceladus's ocean before they figure out the human species.

"And Shashi didn't intervene?"

"He went along with it. You have to know that the men in my family, the Paramara, believe that they're descended from some mythical Agnivansha dynasty. Something made up about their having Aryan blood.

"He was like the rest of the men. He was easily manipulated because he admired power. Like these men who employed him. I told Shashi not to align himself with those Gora-sahebs. I warned him. He was their Gunga Din. But he wouldn't listen."

"But Shashi told me that you want Hindi to prevail in India. Sounds to me that you are a traditionalist as well."

"Hindi is the language of India, but we have a younger generation of Techies who view English as the way to get ahead. English is the language of globalization. Swallowing up cultures like Pac-Man." He noticed that she spoke English with a British accent. "One hundred and ninety-one Indian languages are threatened because of globalization. We must draw a red line at Hindi."

She rose. "My family is really going to be surprised by Shashi's funeral request."

"I hope that you won't be offended by what I have to say."

"Shoot."

"You're a very beautiful woman. Yet your own family is upset by your black skin. It doesn't add up."

"It's the English affect. They infected our country with their social disease which they carry throughout the world. Indians spend billions on skin lightener. They might be the most racist people in the world. I didn't have it as bad as some of the Blacks at the caste bottom. My family had money. I received a good education. But I was lucky in one way. My father gave up on marrying me off. My brother Shashi was one of the few who challenged the racist taunts that I received from my relatives. But in the end he was more British than Indian. Adored Churchill. Churchill said 'I hate Indians. They are a beastly people with a beastly religion.'"

"But doesn't the caste system predate the invasion of the British East India Tea Company? In fact the caste system is thousands of years old so you can't blame it on the White man. Also, Hindi is the language of the Brahman class. The ruling class. You could say that if English is the language of imperialism then Hindi is also the language of an elite. The Brahmins have kept the Dalits down. At least in the American South many Blacks are able to rise to the middle class and even higher. In India, class lines are frozen. It was the Brahmins who have kept the other castes down. Prohibiting literacy among the Untouchables. Why, I've even read that acquisition of education by the Dalits is punishable by cutting off their tongues or by pouring molten lead into the ear of the offender."

"Well, the caste system is thousands of years old, but it was the British who hardened the caste lines. Before they arrived, there was mobility available for different castes. Moreover, some of us Brahmins are different. My group, *Bhaasha Svatantrata*, has done missionary work among the Dalit. Teaching their kids Hindi."

"Yes, Shashi told me, but why isn't this another form of imperialism? Maybe they don't want your values. Maybe they don't want to be Hinduized. As a matter of fact I've read that many Dalits are turning to Islam to insure the safety of their women, who are used as prostitutes by Brahmin men."

"Oh, you think that Muslim men treat their wives differently? Go read Samina Ali's *Madras on Rainy Days*. It'll be easy for you. It's written in English." He ignored the dig.

"While you might dismiss English as the language of Imperialism, the Dalits have a god of English. They worship English."

"Be serious."

He showed her a clipping from *The Telegraph*, a newspaper published in the U.K. (October 27, 2010):

"India's downtrodden 'untouchables' are to open a temple to a 'Goddess of the English language' in honour of Lord Macaulay, an architect of the British Empire. Leaders of India's low-caste Dalits are to celebrate the opening of a temple shaped like a desktop computer to inspire 'untouchable' children to improve their prospects in life by learning English.

"If you were a real radical you would desert your Brahmin comrades and become a Sikh. They don't recognize caste. They reject class, gender, or race-based distinctions between humans. Women are equal to men in Sikhism. If you really wanted to make a statement about women's equality, you would join them." She really got angry. Rose up from where she had been seated.

"Those turban-headed unshaven bastards killed Indira Gandhi, a Brahmin!" She had her hands on her hips and leaned forward. She was hot. Overheated in fact. If it were a 1940s movie, he would have grabbed her and kissed her passionately. She would have struggled momentarily but then submitted. In those days, no meant yes. As late as 1964, in the movie *The Killers*, Ronald Reagan gave Angie Dickenson a hard slap when she refused to follow his demands. But these were the 2000s. You just about had to consult a lawyer before kissing a woman and get the approval of a committee before having sex with her. No longer a problem for Boa. After his prostate surgery, Boa's copulatory organ had been disabled. Put out of commission. Chances of getting an erection was 50/50. If Brigitte and her crew returned, his attitude would be that of the singer in Perry Bradford's "Keep A-Knockin' But-You-Can't-Come-In."

Boa said, "Only after Operation Blue Star October 31, 1984. Indira Gandhi ordered an attack on the Golden Temple, a religious center for Sikhs at Amritsar, Punjab. Hundreds of Sikhs were murdered. Then two Sikh bodyguards, Satwant Singh and Beant Singh, assassinated her as a reprisal. Afterwards Hindus went on a rampage burning down Sikh homes, raping Sikh women and clubbing others to death. Did law enforcement try to stop it? No, like the law enforcement in the United States when White mobs set upon Blacks, they stood by or participated in the carnage."

"That's ridiculous. You believe that because you took an online course in Hindi and hung around with my brother you got India nailed. Just like you Americans. Authorities on everything."

"I have every right to be concerned. Many Indians in this country have been assimilated into the far-Right and are being used against Black Americans. They're introducing Chaturvarna into the country. To them, we are Untouchables. Maybe Si, your progressive Prime Minister, would have ended this Brahminism, which is based upon some mythical invasion of India by Aryans. Based upon a lie."

"He meant well, but unifying Pakistan and India would only mean more patriarchal tyranny!!! Besides, you may criticize my caste, but the way I look at it, you're a Brahmin."

"That's ridiculous."

"Well you live quite differently than those poor people who were consumed by fire on San Pablo. You live in this posh neighborhood while they lived in squalor. They're your Dalits."

"That's so far-fetched. Where did you get that from?"

"Follow my argument. You and your class hate the new president, yet his administration's plan to cut corporate taxes has boosted the stock market. Adding revenue to your portfolio. True?" He thought about that one. He rarely consulted his portfolio. Had problems with figuring out the stock symbols.

But yes, he did receive a nice check yearly from a broker that handled the investments of teachers.

"You and other Black professionals dislike the Übers who are moving into your neighborhoods, but look at it this way. How long have you had this house?"

"Maybe a year?"

"Because of their presence, the property values in this neighborhood have gone up. This house is probably worth double the price that you paid for it. Positively, Brahman. And you're complaining about their dog poop?"

His mind was like a basketball player who got into a fast break but whose slam dunk failed. He tried hard to come up with a rebuttal. The harder he tried the angrier he became. There was silence. "Shashi told me that you were reading the ancient myths of India, designed by an elite patriarchal group of male priests. You should read Pakistani and Indian women writers. They are creating new sheroes. New stories."

She finished her chai. "Not bad." She walked over to him and pinched him on the cheek. "You look cute when you're mad." She sped away on her motorcycle.

Chapter Thirty-three

BOWING TO HER SUGGESTION, he Kindled some books by Indian and Pakistani women writers. He spent the weekend reading them. He couldn't believe what he was reading. Though Black American men had become international pariahs as a result of the "girlfriend" books, Bogeyman theater, and television, directed, produced, and with scripts written as well as published by men, mostly, who'd never been profiled, racially, or red-lined. But if Black men pulled some of the shit against women that Pakistani and Indian men get away with, they'd be shot or find their baths interrupted by someone pouring scalding hot grits on them. In these novels and short stories wives and daughters are property. In Chitra Banerjee Divakaruni's short story "The Bats," a Calcutta mother and child are constantly abused by the husband and father. They repeatedly leave home only to return to suffer more abuse. Their situation is compared with that of bats who attack the child's granduncle's orchard. The granduncle finally resorts to using poison. The next day the ground is littered with the corpses of bats, yet the bats keep returning. In "Clothes," it is proffered that a married woman "belongs to her husband and her in-laws." In "Silver Pavements; Golden Roofs," Jayanti tries to liberate her aunt who has been lured into an arranged marriage by the promise that her husband is the head of an automobile empire, when he is actually a mechanic working in a dingy shop. He has placed her in virtual house arrest and so when Jayanti persuades her to take a walk through the streets of Chicago, where both of them are called "niggers" by some White kids, Jayanti's uncle

185

threatens to beat her. She can't get over the White kids calling her a nigger. She says:

> . . . can't they see that I'm not black at all but an Indian girl of good family? When our chauffeur Gurbans Singh drives me down the Calcutta streets in our silver-colored Fiat, people stop to whisper, "Isn't that Jayanti Ganguli, daughter of the Bhavanipur Gangulis?"

In *The Upstairs Wife: An Intimate History of Pakistan* by Rafia Zakaria, a woman, Amina, is married to a man, Sonail, who takes a second wife whom he loves more than her. Page after page shows her humiliation and neglect. To add to that, the wives live in the same house. She lives upstairs and the second wife downstairs. After the second wife dies, the first wife suggests that she and her husband move to the first floor, where the second wife resided. "Then he cleared his throat and with the softest of voices poured out in words venom more deathly than blows. 'You know, Amina, twenty years ago when I married her, I learned for the first time what it was to be happy, to be with someone I truly understood and who truly understood me . . .

"'I could have left you then, as so many men do. We did not have children and your father could have given you a home.' He stared at Amina, her face flushed as if freshly slapped, glassy, and his lips wet. 'I did not leave you because I did not want you to be disgraced, to live like an abandoned woman.'"

A woman who has been abandoned by her husband is discarded to a human trash heap, like Henna in Samina Ali's *Madras on Rainy Days*, where it is said, "A girl raised without a father, without a man's name shielding her reputation, might as well be illegitimate, might as well be a whore." Widows don't fare much better. In Chitra Divakaruni's "Clothes," after her husband Somesh is killed in America in a hold-up, her in-laws invite Sumita to return to India to be their daughter for life. For her, widows in India are "Doves with cut-off wings."

"That's when I know I cannot go back. I don't know yet how I'll manage, here in this new, dangerous land. I only know I must. Because all over India, at this very moment, widows in white saris are bowing their veiled heads, serving tea to in-laws. Doves with cut-off wings." He read on as these women told their stories.

In Jamila Hashmi's "Banishment," which is included in the anthology *So That You Can Know Me* edited by Yasmin Hameed and Asif Aslam Farrukii, Bibi, the wife of Gurpal, becomes the slave of his grandmother, Badi Ma. Her husband calls Bibi "a maidservant" and tells her to make his wife "grind the millstone and fetch water from the well. You can order her to do anything you want." In Zaitoon Bano's "Dilshad," Dilshad is sold to her husband by her father for fifteen hundred rupees. After her husband is murdered, his eldest brother takes her in marriage by force and beats her mercilessly.

On KPFA, Berkeley, he'd heard that an Egyptian woman had read bell hooks, one of the country's bravest intellectuals, and, as a result, corners of her brain that were inert were activated. The media had given White women credit for doing all of the feminist thinking, but he got the impression that women in China, the Middle East, India, and Africa were inspired by Black women writers. Maybe it was because White women had accompanied the invaders who plundered their countries' resources. Brutalized and raped the natives. Tolerated genocide.

Collaborators. In the United States, they even bought Black women. In her "Mistresses of the Market: White Women and the Nineteenth-Century Domestic Slave Trade," Dr. Stephanie Jones-Rogers, University of California Berkeley, proposed that the image of the slave master as a male, exclusively, was inaccurate. White Southern women participated in the commerce as well. Sometimes buying Black women who were forced to entertain White men in Southern brothels. It was German, Polish, French, and other European women who collaborated with the Nazis and stood by and cheered as their Jewish sisters and their children were shoved into ovens.

Boa found it puzzling that men from other ethnic groups joined academic feminists in an attack on Black men. It's like Jewish producers and writers like David Simon, David Mamet, and Steven Spielberg producing Black feminist products, or mediating the dispute between Black men and women, yet neglecting the plight of Jewish American women in the United States or Israel, where they sit in the back on buses and get stoned if they wear clothes disapproved of by Orthodox Jews.

Boa dozed off with one of the books lying on his chest. He was in that region of consciousness between awake and asleep. Monroe Trotter was sitting next to his bed. He tried to wake up but couldn't. Trotter was shaking his head, sadly.

"I ask myself, was it worth it? The sacrifices that me, DuBois, and others made. I went to jail and he had his passport revoked because we stood up for our beliefs. And what was the outcome. A consumerist middle class whose only ambition is to be in front of the line at Thanksgiving and Christmas sales. All night drinking in Paris followed by a breakfast of oysters. Yellow roadsters that can reach 150 miles per hour. Sixty-five-inch color TV screens. Rampant hedonism. Cashing in on slavery. All of our work coming to naught. My Phi Beta Kappa ring. Means nothing. Our work on the Niagara Movement, nothing. Integration—a shallow Utopian dream. Our generation regarded justice and fair play as the American Way. What is the American Way nowadays? How does Three 6 Mafia, a hip-hop group explain it? *Smoke all night, sleep all day / That's the epitome of the American way / Roll that shit, light that shit, hit that shit, hold that shit / Blow that shit out slow, then pass it to me bro.* Disgusting.

"What did all of our protest against *Birth of a Nation* lead to? This monstrous insult is now considered a classic. Ranks 44 among the 100 great films selected by the American Film Institute. Has wider distribution than ever before because of streaming services. My contesting Woodrow Wilson's eliminating Blacks from the Civil Service? Wilson is still honored at Princeton. How many of your Black students ever heard of Black Reconstruction? And then we had such hopes for Africa. India. Such promise. But in Eritrea, Zimbabwe, Congo, petty dictators who won't let go. Who are owned by corporations that are beyond government and have assumed the status of persons. To think I went to Paris, posing as a chef to try to get some human rights provisions into the League of Nations. A failure. Twenty-one African countries are now headed by dictators whose pockets are being stuffed by multi-nationals. They don't care if millions starve as a result of man-made famines, caused by greediness of the global North. They've been bought off. South African currency downgraded to junk, after all the sacrifices made by Mandela. Our people were lynched, even massacred for the right to vote. What do our descendants do? Stay home. And now this man. A public intellectual. An entertainer. Making money by becoming an expert on me. I could have used that money to sustain my newspaper, *The Guardian*. Slavery has become a sideshow. Torture porn. Oppression chic. Yes I had issues with DuBois and Booker T. Washington but if they were around to witness what became of our dreams, they would be appalled." With that, he vanished before Boa could tell him, "Africa has become a destination for doing world-class science. Gabon, Zambia, Uganda, Cameroon, Ivory Coast, Congo, Tanzania, Ghana, Ethiopia, Kenya, and Angola have a higher GDP than the United States."

By this time in his life, he thought he'd be a Babaji or a *ologbon okunrin*, or have reached *satyagraha*, "truth force, love force, soul force." Instead he was cashing in on slavery chic and entertainment and servicing Brigitte and her posse. He was wasting his life. The species was on the verge of extinction, yet a whole industry had developed around an immersion in the past. For cash. What was that Burt Bacharach lyric? "A fool will lose tomorrow reaching back for yesterday." We were all fools as the sixth extinction was underway.

Chapter Thirty-four

SHASHI'S FUNERAL WAS TELEVISED on C-SPAN. Badaboodaar Saanp, this mouse-faced *Maadher chod*, delivered the eulogy. Had little biddy beady nerdy eyes and his hair glued to his scalp. He was introduced as president of the Gunga Din Society, an Indian organization whose members were right-wing members of the media, academia, think tanks, and the Neo-Nazi administration. The FCC chairman for example and the woman in charge of gutting Medicaid. Calling Shashi the brightest of his protégés; he almost broke down. Like Shashi, he was member of a family that converted to Anglicanism so as to cultivate British commercial contacts. His attacks on Black Americans had been laced with a vicious sarcasm.

"I suspect that all of those on the left are satisfied now that the young man who did the most to convince Americans that, as Robert E. Lee said, it was the White people who suffered the most from slavery, is now dead. It is the Blacks that should be paying the descendants of the slave owners who put these people up, took care of them, improved their blood line, while they partied all of the time and made bets on Camptown races. He will certainly be missed. And yes, he suffered abuse that we Indians in think tanks, universities, on editorial boards are subjected to by followers of the latest hothead, Si, who embarrassed us all over the world, and some of the Hindu nationalists who are even sitting here in this church." With that he paused and stared at Kala who was sitting in the front row. She crossed her arms and gave him the look that one would a cockroach that suddenly crossed one's dinner plate.

"They call we Anglo Indians Gunga Dins, which is supposed be a term of condemnation, but do you know what, I accept the term. For Anglo Indians everywhere, I say proudly that I am Gunga Din. We are New Gunga Dins, no longer 'black-faced squidgy-nosed' Barbarians, but educated at the best Western universities, sophisticated and willing to give up our lives for Christian civilization, and if we die we will die proudly having achieved this task. We will accept the bullet for this noble cause and die with those immortal lines from Gunga Din, 'I 'ope you liked your drink, Sir.'"

This line was greeted with sustained round of applause by some of Shashi's right-wing Indian colleagues. In fact, as their White sponsors rose in unison, they continued as he lengthened his conceit. "We 'limping lump o' brick-dust' stand soldier to soldier with those who defend our values. Our western values, lying with 'bricky-dry' throats in a battle with heathen, we gladly rush to their aid with our 'goatskin water-bag.' We will plug our comrades where they bleed. And as we die we will say like Gunga Din said, I 'ope you liked your drink. I 'ope you liked your drink, Sir.'"

He repeated the phrase until he was joined by the Indians and their millionaire and billionaire funders. At first they sat. Then they rose again and kept repeating the phrase. When they sat down he said, dramatically looking down at Shashi's casket, "And I am sure that Shashi, our martyr, if he were with me would also say, 'I 'ope you liked your drink, Sir.'"

The applause went on for five minutes during which Kala stood up and left the church. Her mother tried to go after her, maybe give her a slap for leaving the church, but she was so weighed down in an expensive sari and jewels, she couldn't rise from her seat.

Boa was sitting in the back. After the family and procession left he got up and walked out into the New York sun. Past the long line of funeral cars that included Rolls Royces and Jaguars belonging to Shashi's right-wing supporters. If he had finished his remarks instead of being shot, they wouldn't have shown up. They would have been shocked to hear that he had changed. What was on Boa's mind? What was he thinking? Was he going to continue to receive money from the slavery debates and who was going to replace Shashi?

Momentarily the coffin was carried out. Complying with Shashi's requests, six women dressed as cowgirls wearing identical Dale Evans outfits were carrying the coffin. Gently. Walking behind them was a tall Black Jazz musician, dressed in a Gene Autry outfit. You know, that beautiful piece, "Water," by Roy Rogers's Sons of the Pioneers. He could tell that Badaboodaar Saanp and his entourage were furious. Shashi wanted that in his funeral. A nod to the Oakland drought. Shashi wanted a funeral that a 2017 Krishna would approve of.

The family was last to depart from the church. They joined Kala, who was already outside, having left the church during Saanp's speech. She wore a black dress, hat, black shoes—the traditional garb of mourning. Boa climbed into his rented car. He purposely chose a convertible, the color of a red pepper to symbolize Shashi's erotic side. But what did their adventures come to? They were 'hos. Pure and simple. He was thinking how he was going to spend the rest of his life. Maybe Tritone was right that he was a walking oversized black dildo. Would he spend the rest of his life in pursuit of noble things. Ideas. As the Schwarzenegger would say ". . . and things of that nature." He was rummaging through his thoughts when he heard some commotion in the front of the funeral procession. It was coming from the lead car, which contained Shashi's family. A BMW station wagon. Shashi's sister jumped out of the car. She seemed to be arguing with its occupants. She then, with her arms folded, and her head held high, began to walk in the street down the line of cars. When she came alongside his, he rolled down a window. "*Maiy tumhay chai pur bulaanaa chaa hutaa hoon?*" She stood there for a minute.

"Yes I'll go with you for a cup of chai as long as you don't try to speak Hindi. You mangle it."

"So what was that all about back there?"

"Oh, my family. So racist. So backward. They were upset about Shashi's funeral requests. The cowherd girls and most of all Krishna, represented by a Black gender-reassigned musician. They hate Jazz. They're so fucking Brahmin."

Shashi's family belonged to the Anglican Church, but were Hindus in their souls. His Dad made a show of accepting a foreign religion in order to profit from their English business connections. When they entertained some British visitors they hid the Hindu icons and placed prominent photos of the Archbishop of Canterbury and crosses in their stead. When asked to explain the "pagan" statues lining the path leading to the main house, they'd explain that the statues were there when they bought the house and that to remove them would offend the superstitious peasants who lived in the village. By her expressions regarding her family, he knew that Kala could never return to India. She would join a growing list of Pakistani and Indian women who found it easier to critique India's especially cruel patriarchy from America, where their independence was accepted more than at home. Of course, some of the women still lived under Old City rules, but others had a choice. Would Kala follow the lead of Bharati Mukherjee, and Elizabeth Nunez, who acknowledged that it was traditional Black Americans whose 400-year-old resistance made it easier for the colored immigrants to advance in American society? Would they advance even over those whose sacrifices had made the society more tolerant? Who were lynched and assassinated as a result of their challenging the premise that American society should be the White man's playpen?

Black journalists like Robert Maynard had challenged the Jim Crow media. The Jim Crow media had responded by awarding positions to those who weren't born here, while firing the few traditional Black Americans to whom they gave spots.

Traditional African Americans had fought to include Ethnic Studies at American universities, even though a Hispanic writer who suffered from what might be called a Black Erasure Amnesia refused to give them credit.

So why did the apprentice colonialists who run the media and academia prefer foreign-born and second-generation personnel to traditional African Americans? Gerald Horne says it's because traditional Black Americans will never be forgiven for siding with the British against the slaveholders in the so-called American Revolution which he says, convincingly, was fought so that the slave owners could keep their slaves. There might be another reason. Were these educated immigrants addicted to White supremacy? The feisty Mayadevi, a Hindu woman in Bulbul Sharma's "Mayadevi's London Yatra," on her way to London to visit her son, was told by an airline hostess that she found Indian people, even the poor ones, so kind and possessing "large hearts." The elderly Mayadevi answered, "Why they not be kind? They lick white people's shoes 200 years and now it becomes bad habit like drinking and smoking." Was that it? That these immigrants had been so domesticated by their colonial masters over 200 years that they had become their pupils? How did V. T. Rajshekar put it? "The slaves have started enjoying slavery."

He figured that he and Kala had a lot of conjugating ahead of them. You know, helping Boa with his pronunciations and stuff. His distinguishing between gender pronouns. No longer did he have to worry about Brigitte and her gang. They hadn't been around. She probably had gotten the word of his new anatomical status. He thought of all of the scholarly women and intellectuals who could have broadened his perspective. But after having sex with them, his relationship with them soured.

He wouldn't let that happen with Kala. They would have lengthy discussions as she explained Postcolonial theory to him. Or why India shouldn't move away from the Devanagari script. And maybe she could find him a discount rate for a trip to Bharti. The car peeled off from the rest of the funeral caravan. They were taking the body back to India. Kala would remain behind. They headed downtown. On East Sixth Street, which was lined with Indian restaurants, the traffic was bumper to bumper. There was a downpour. Kala had snuggled up against him. He thought of what the Doctor had said about the chances of getting an erection, as 50/50. Not bad odds. Maybe while Kala helped him conjugate Hindi, he could conjugate Kala. But Tritone appeared in his head. He was pointing his finger at Boa and shaking his head. Boa agreed. His days of decadence were behind him.

As he was waiting to move on and find a parking space, he had a weird feeling. He turned and staring at him was an Indian boy. He was standing on the curb with his parents. The three began crossing the street. When they came in front of the rent-a-car, the child turned to Boa's car and shouted.

"Hey, Boa, I got Mexico!" The child's mother yanked his hand so they could continue crossing to the other side of the street. Once there, the child turned again to Boa and rendered a deep smile. He waved until he and his parents disappeared into the crowds of young people strolling up and down the streets of the Lower East Side. Stunned, Boa couldn't move. He sat behind the wheel, frozen. The cars behind him began to honk. The speedometer was at zero. Kala turned to him.

"Anything wrong?" she asked.

End

ISHMAEL REED is the author of over twenty-five books, including *Mumbo Jumbo*, *The Last Days of Louisiana Red*, *Yellow Back Radio Broke-Down*, and *Juice!*. He is also a publisher, television producer, songwriter, radio and television commentator, lecturer, and has long been devoted to exploring an alternative black aesthetic: the trickster tradition, or Neo-Hoodooism as he calls it. Founder of the Before Columbus Foundation, he taught at the University of California, Berkeley, for over thirty years, retiring in 2005. In 2003, he received the coveted Otto Award for political theater.

MICHAL AJVAZ, *The Golden Age.*
The Other City.
PIERRE ALBERT-BIROT, *Grabinoulor.*
YUZ ALESHKOVSKY, *Kangaroo.*
SVETLANA ALEXIEVICH, *Voices from Chernobyl.*
FELIPE ALFAU, *Chromos.*
Locos.
JOAO ALMINO, *Enigmas of Spring.*
IVAN ÂNGELO, *The Celebration.*
The Tower of Glass.
ANTÓNIO LOBO ANTUNES, *Knowledge of Hell.*
The Splendor of Portugal.
ALAIN ARIAS-MISSON, *Theatre of Incest.*
JOHN ASHBERY & JAMES SCHUYLER, *A Nest of Ninnies.*
GABRIELA AVIGUR-ROTEM, *Heatwave and Crazy Birds.*
DJUNA BARNES, *Ladies Almanack.*
Ryder.
JOHN BARTH, *Letters.*
Sabbatical.
Collected Stories.
DONALD BARTHELME, *The King.*
Paradise.
SVETISLAV BASARA, *Chinese Letter.*
Fata Morgana.
In Search of the Grail.
MIQUEL BAUÇÀ, *The Siege in the Room.*
RENÉ BELLETTO, *Dying.*
MAREK BIEŃCZYK, *Transparency.*
ANDREI BITOV, *Pushkin House.*
ANDREJ BLATNIK, *You Do Understand.*
Law of Desire.
LOUIS PAUL BOON, *Chapel Road.*
My Little War.
Summer in Termuren.
ROGER BOYLAN, *Killoyle.*
IGNÁCIO DE LOYOLA BRANDÃO, *Anonymous Celebrity.*
Zero.
BRIGID BROPHY, *In Transit.*
The Prancing Novelist.

GABRIELLE BURTON, *Heartbreak Hotel.*
MICHEL BUTOR, *Degrees.*
Mobile.
G. CABRERA INFANTE, *Infante's Inferno.*
Three Trapped Tigers.
JULIETA CAMPOS, *The Fear of Losing Eurydice.*
ANNE CARSON, *Eros the Bittersweet.*
ORLY CASTEL-BLOOM, *Dolly City.*
LOUIS-FERDINAND CÉLINE, *North.*
Conversations with Professor Y.
London Bridge.
HUGO CHARTERIS, *The Tide Is Right.*
ERIC CHEVILLARD, *Demolishing Nisard.*
The Author and Me.
MARC CHOLODENKO, *Mordechai Schamz.*
EMILY HOLMES COLEMAN, *The Shutter of Snow.*
ERIC CHEVILLARD, *The Author and Me.*
LUIS CHITARRONI, *The No Variations.*
CH'OE YUN, *Mannequin.*
ROBERT COOVER, *A Night at the Movies.*
STANLEY CRAWFORD, *Log of the S.S.*
The Mrs Unguentine.
Some Instructions to My Wife.
RALPH CUSACK, *Cadenza.*
NICHOLAS DELBANCO *Sherbrookes.*
The Count of Concord.
NIGEL DENNIS, *Cards of Identity.*
PETER DIMOCK, *A Short Rhetoric for Leaving the Family.*
ARIEL DORFMAN, *Konfidenz.*
COLEMAN DOWELL, *Island People.*
Too Much Flesh and Jabez.
RIKKI DUCORNET, *Phosphor in Dreamland.*
The Complete Butcher's Tales.
RIKKI DUCORNET (corr.), *The Jade Cabinet.*
The Fountains of Neptune.
WILLIAM EASTLAKE, *Castle Keep.*
Lyric of the Circle Heart.
JEAN ECHENOZ, *Chopin's Move.*

STANLEY ELKIN, *A Bad Man*.
The Dick Gibson Show.
The Franchiser.

FRANÇOIS EMMANUEL, *Invitation to a Voyage*.

SALVADOR ESPRIU, *Ariadne in the Grotesque Labyrinth*.

LESLIE A. FIEDLER, *Love and Death in the American Novel*.

JUAN FILLOY, *Op Oloop*.

GUSTAVE FLAUBERT, *Bouvard and Pécuchet*.

JON FOSSE, *Aliss at the Fire*.
Melancholy.
Trilogy.

FORD MADOX FORD, *The March of Literature*.

MAX FRISCH, *I'm Not Stiller*.
Man in the Holocene.

CARLOS FUENTES, *Christopher Unborn*.
Distant Relations.
Terra Nostra.
Where the Air Is Clear.
Nietzsche on His Balcony.

WILLIAM GADDIS, JR., *The Recognitions*.
JR.

JANICE GALLOWAY, *Foreign Parts*.
The Trick Is to Keep Breathing.

WILLIAM H. GASS, *Life Sentences*.
The Tunnel.
The World Within the Word.
Willie Masters' Lonesome Wife.

GÉRARD GAVARRY, *Hoppla! 1 2 3*.

ETIENNE GILSON, *The Arts of the Beautiful*.
Forms and Substances in the Arts.

C. S. GISCOMBE, *Giscome Road*.
Here.

DOUGLAS GLOVER, *Bad News of the Heart*.

WITOLD GOMBROWICZ, *A Kind of Testament*.

PAULO EMÍLIO SALES GOMES, *P's Three Women*.

GEORGI GOSPODINOV, *Natural Novel*.

JUAN GOYTISOLO, *Juan the Landless*.
Makbara.
Marks of Identity.

JACK GREEN, *Fire the Bastards!*

JIŘÍ GRUŠA, *The Questionnaire*.

MELA HARTWIG, *Am I a Redundant Human Being?*

JOHN HAWKES, *The Passion Artist*.
Whistlejacket.

ELIZABETH HEIGHWAY, ED., *Contemporary Georgian Fiction*.

AIDAN HIGGINS, *Balcony of Europe*.
Blind Man's Bluff.
Bornholm Night-Ferry.
Langrishe, Go Down.
Scenes from a Receding Past.

ALDOUS HUXLEY, *Antic Hay*.
Point Counter Point.
Those Barren Leaves.
Time Must Have a Stop.

JANG JUNG-IL, *When Adam Opens His Eyes*

DRAGO JANČAR, *The Tree with No Name*.
I Saw Her That Night.
Galley Slave.

MIKHEIL JAVAKHISHVILI, *Kvachi*.

GERT JONKE, *The Distant Sound*.
Homage to Czerny.
The System of Vienna.

JACQUES JOUET, *Mountain R*.
Savage.
Upstaged.

JUNG YOUNG-MOON, *A Contrived World*.

MIEKO KANAI, *The Word Book*.

YORAM KANIUK, *Life on Sandpaper*.

ZURAB KARUMIDZE, *Dagny*.

PABLO KATCHADJIAN, *What to Do*.

JOHN KELLY, *From Out of the City*.

HUGH KENNER, *Flaubert, Joyce and Beckett: The Stoic Comedians*.
Joyce's Voices.

DANILO KIŠ, *The Attic*.
The Lute and the Scars.
Psalm 44.
A Tomb for Boris Davidovich.

ANITA KONKKA, *A Fool's Paradise*.

GEORGE KONRÁD, *The City Builder.*

TADEUSZ KONWICKI, *A Minor Apocalypse.*
The Polish Complex.

ELAINE KRAF, *The Princess of 72nd Street.*

JIM KRUSOE, *Iceland.*

AYSE KULIN, *Farewell: A Mansion in Occupied Istanbul.*

EMILIO LASCANO TEGUI, *On Elegance While Sleeping.*

ERIC LAURRENT, *Do Not Touch.*

VIOLETTE LEDUC, *La Bâtarde.*

LEE KI-HO, *At Least We Can Apologize.*

EDOUARD LEVÉ, *Autoportrait.*
Suicide.

MARIO LEVI, *Istanbul Was a Fairy Tale.*

DEBORAH LEVY, *Billy and Girl.*

JOSÉ LEZAMA LIMA, *Paradiso.*

OSMAN LINS, *Avalovara.*
The Queen of the Prisons of Greece.

ALF MACLOCHLAINN, *Out of Focus.*
Past Habitual.

RON LOEWINSOHN, *Magnetic Field(s).*

YURI LOTMAN, *Non-Memoirs.*

D. KEITH MANO, *Take Five.*

MINA LOY, *Stories and Essays of Mina Loy.*

MICHELINE AHARONIAN MARCOM, *The Mirror in the Well.*

BEN MARCUS, *The Age of Wire and String.*

WALLACE MARKFIELD, *Teitlebaum's Window.*
To an Early Grave.

DAVID MARKSON, *Reader's Block.*
Wittgenstein's Mistress.

CAROLE MASO, *AVA.*

HISAKI MATSUURA, *Triangle.*

LADISLAV MATEJKA & KRYSTYNA POMORSKA, EDS., *Readings in Russian Poetics: Formalist & Structuralist Views.*

HARRY MATHEWS, *Cigarettes.*
The Conversions.
The Human Country.
The Journalist.
My Life in CIA.

Singular Pleasures.
The Sinking of the Odradek Stadium.
Tlooth.

JOSEPH MCELROY, *Night Soul and Other Stories.*

ABDELWAHAB MEDDEB, *Talismano.*

GERHARD MEIER, *Isle of the Dead.*

HERMAN MELVILLE, *The Confidence-Man.*

AMANDA MICHALOPOULOU, *I'd Like.*

STEVEN MILLHAUSER, *The Barnum Museum.*
In the Penny Arcade.

RALPH J. MILLS, JR., *Essays on Poetry.*

CHRISTINE MONTALBETTI, *The Origin of Man.*
Western.

NICHOLAS MOSLEY, *Accident.*
Assassins.
Catastrophe Practice.
Hopeful Monsters.
Imago Bird.
Natalie Natalia.
Serpent.

WARREN MOTTE, *Fiction Now: The French Novel in the 21st Century.*
Oulipo: A Primer of Potential Literature.

GERALD MURNANE, *Barley Patch.*
Inland.

YVES NAVARRE, *Our Share of Time.*
Sweet Tooth.

DOROTHY NELSON, *In Night's City.*
Tar and Feathers.

WILFRIDO D. NOLLEDO, *But for the Lovers.*

BORIS A. NOVAK, *The Master of Insomnia.*

FLANN O'BRIEN, *At Swim-Two-Birds.*
The Best of Myles.
The Dalkey Archive.
The Hard Life.
The Poor Mouth.
The Third Policeman.

CLAUDE OLLIER, *The Mise-en-Scène.*
Wert and the Life Without End.

PATRIK OUŘEDNÍK, *Europeana.*
The Opportune Moment, 1855.
BORIS PAHOR, *Necropolis.*
FERNANDO DEL PASO, *News from the Empire.*
Palinuro of Mexico.
ROBERT PINGET, *The Inquisitory.*
Mahu or The Material.
Trio.
MANUEL PUIG, *Betrayed by Rita Hayworth.*
The Buenos Aires Affair.
Heartbreak Tango.
RAYMOND QUENEAU, *The Last Days.*
Odile.
Pierrot Mon Ami.
Saint Glinglin.
ANN QUIN, *Berg.*
Passages.
Three.
Tripticks.
ISHMAEL REED, *The Free-Lance Pallbearers.*
The Last Days of Louisiana Red.
Ishmael Reed: The Plays.
Juice!
The Terrible Threes.
The Terrible Twos.
Yellow Back Radio Broke-Down.
RAINER MARIA RILKE,
The Notebooks of Malte Laurids Brigge.
JULIÁN RÍOS, *The House of Ulysses.*
Larva: A Midsummer Night's Babel.
Poundemonium.
ALAIN ROBBE-GRILLET, *Project for a Revolution in New York.*
A Sentimental Novel.
AUGUSTO ROA BASTOS, *I the Supreme.*
DANIËL ROBBERECHTS, *Arriving in Avignon.*
JEAN ROLIN, *The Explosion of the Radiator Hose.*
OLIVIER ROLIN, *Hotel Crystal.*
ALIX CLEO ROUBAUD, *Alix's Journal.*
JACQUES ROUBAUD, *The Form of a City Changes Faster, Alas, Than the Human Heart.*

The Great Fire of London.
Hortense in Exile.
Hortense Is Abducted.
Mathematics: The Plurality of Worlds of Lewis.
Some Thing Black.
RAYMOND ROUSSEL, *Impressions of Africa.*
VEDRANA RUDAN, *Night.*
GERMAN SADULAEV, *The Maya Pill.*
TOMAŽ ŠALAMUN, *Soy Realidad.*
LYDIE SALVAYRE, *The Company of Ghosts.*
LUIS RAFAEL SÁNCHEZ, *Macho Camacho's Beat.*
SEVERO SARDUY, *Cobra & Maitreya.*
NATHALIE SARRAUTE, *Do You Hear Them?*
Martereau.
The Planetarium.
STIG SÆTERBAKKEN, *Siamese.*
Self-Control.
Through the Night.
ARNO SCHMIDT, *Collected Novellas.*
Collected Stories.
Nobodaddy's Children.
Two Novels.
ASAF SCHURR, *Motti.*
GAIL SCOTT, *My Paris.*
JUNE AKERS SEESE,
Is This What Other Women Feel Too?
BERNARD SHARE, *Inish.*
Transit.
VIKTOR SHKLOVSKY, *Bowstring.*
Literature and Cinematography.
Theory of Prose.
Third Factory.
Zoo, or Letters Not about Love.
PIERRE SINIAC, *The Collaborators.*
KJERSTI A. SKOMSVOLD,
The Faster I Walk, the Smaller I Am.
JOSEF ŠKVORECKÝ, *The Engineer of Human Souls.*
GILBERT SORRENTINO, *Aberration of Starlight.*
Blue Pastoral.
Crystal Vision.

Imaginative Qualities of Actual Things.
Mulligan Stew.
Red the Fiend.
Steelwork.
Under the Shadow.
ANDRZEJ STASIUK, *Dukla.*
Fado.
GERTRUDE STEIN, *The Making of Americans.*
A Novel of Thank You.
PIOTR SZEWC, *Annihilation.*
GONÇALO M. TAVARES, *A Man: Klaus Klump.*
Jerusalem.
Learning to Pray in the Age of Technique.
LUCIAN DAN TEODOROVICI, *Our Circus Presents . . .*
NIKANOR TERATOLOGEN, *Assisted Living.*
STEFAN THEMERSON, *Hobson's Island.*
The Mystery of the Sardine.
Tom Harris.
JOHN TOOMEY, *Sleepwalker.*
Huddleston Road.
Slipping.
DUMITRU TSEPENEAG, *Hotel Europa.*
The Necessary Marriage.
Pigeon Post.
Vain Art of the Fugue.
La Belle Roumaine.
Waiting: Stories.
ESTHER TUSQUETS, *Stranded.*
DUBRAVKA UGRESIC, *Lend Me Your Character.*
Thank You for Not Reading.
TOR ULVEN, *Replacement.*
MATI UNT, *Brecht at Night.*
Diary of a Blood Donor.
Things in the Night.
ÁLVARO URIBE & OLIVIA SEARS, EDS., *Best of Contemporary Mexican Fiction.*
ELOY URROZ, *Friction.*
The Obstacles.
LUISA VALENZUELA, *Dark Desires and the Others.*
He Who Searches.

PAUL VERHAEGHEN, *Omega Minor.*
BORIS VIAN, *Heartsnatcher.*
TOOMAS VINT, *An Unending Landscape.*
ORNELA VORPSI, *The Country Where No One Ever Dies.*
AUSTRYN WAINHOUSE, *Hedyphagetica.*
MARKUS WERNER, *Cold Shoulder.*
Zundel's Exit.
CURTIS WHITE, *The Idea of Home.*
Memories of My Father Watching TV.
Requiem.
DIANE WILLIAMS, *Excitability: Selected Stories.*
DOUGLAS WOOLF, *Wall to Wall.*
Ya! & John-Juan.
JAY WRIGHT, *Polynomials and Pollen.*
The Presentable Art of Reading Absence.
PHILIP WYLIE, *Generation of Vipers.*
MARGUERITE YOUNG, *Angel in the Forest.*
Miss MacIntosh, My Darling.
REYOUNG, *Unbabbling.*
ZORAN ŽIVKOVIĆ , *Hidden Camera.*
LOUIS ZUKOFSKY, *Collected Fiction.*
VITOMIL ZUPAN, *Minuet for Guitar.*
SCOTT ZWIREN, *God Head.*

AND MORE . . .